The Stillburrow Crush

by

Linda Kage

The Stillburrow Crush

COPYRIGHT © 2009 by Linda Grotheer

Cover Art by *Kimberlee Mendoza*

The Wild Rose Press
PO Box 706
Adams Basin, NY 14410-0706
Visit us at www.thewildrosepress.com

Publishing History
First Climbing Rose Edition, 2010
Print ISBN 1-60154-651-3

Published in the United States of America

A bead of muddy sweat trickled out of his hairline and down his temple, mixing with blood before moving on. Fascinated, I watched it drool a crooked path down his cheek and neck and then into the collar of his jersey.

As if catching my entranced stare, he lifted the hand that held his helmet and wiped the sweat away with the back of his palm. "What do you want to know?"

I cleared my throat and dropped my eyes. "Umm, well..." I yanked a notebook from the inside pocket of my trench coat. The wind caught a few sheets, making the lined pages flail and thrash like they were drowning in the ocean or something. I tried to get a hold of them and rein them in but only succeeded in wrinkling most of the pad.

"Sorry," I muttered, and dug deep into my outer pocket, frantically searching for my pen. I couldn't find the irritating thing there, and switched hands on the notebook to search the other pocket. I didn't dare look up. I could feel *him* watching and it made my cheeks hot.

He coughed, trying to get my attention, and my head flew up—long bangs falling into my eyes. He motioned toward my right ear with his index finger. I frowned, wondering if there was a twig or something in my hair and reached up, patting the area. And the pen, which had been securely tucked behind my ear, stabbed me.

"Ouch!"

Dedication

For Sandra

Chapter One

I couldn't believe it. Not until I was standing there along with the rest of the town in the cemetery did it really hit me. She was dead.

It'd been a drunk-driving accident and she'd been the one drinking while driving her dad's Lexus. The ironic part was her mother headed the town's MADD program. No one seemed to think the irony of it was too awfully funny, though.

Her best friend, Jill, wasn't there. She was laid up in the hospital thirty miles away with a broken hipbone and other injuries. She'd been in the passenger's seat. But pretty much everyone else had shown. Even the Wallaces made an appearance, and they were the couple who'd sideswiped her when she'd run the stop sign and pulled out in front of them. They'd managed to come through the accident with only minor bumps and bruises. Mrs. Wallace held her arm in a sling and her husband, the town's dentist, sported a black eye.

I couldn't look at the closed casket with its mountain of flowers piled on top. So I stared down the street to where the school sat only a block away. From where I stood, I could see the massive brick walls rising above house and tree.

The path from Fitz's Funeral Home to the cemetery went directly past the school. As I stared, I could remember when I was younger and a funeral line would pass by during recess. All the children, me included, would line the edge of the playground and count the number of cars in the procession. If the number was too few, we'd shrug and say, "Guess no one liked Old Man Roper much, did they?" or something to that effect. Then we'd go back to playing tag or jumping rope.

When I was in second grade, my Grandfather Burke died. I was still too young to think much of death back then—or understand it—but I remember looking at my friends from the back seat of my parents' Suburban and wishing the kids at recess would count the biggest number of cars yet.

Standing at Grandpa's graveside service, I could hear my friends at recess. The squeak of swing sets and the laughter of children playing echoed down the street. I tried to be still in my scratchy black wool dress but was incredibly bored. I watched Grandpa's face and wondered why he wasn't snoring like he usually did when he napped. I didn't want to be there in that dreadful dress, in those tight shoes and watch him sleep. I wanted to be down the block, playing at recess. When I grew impatient enough to ask Mom if Grandpa was going to wake up soon so I could go back to school, she clutched my fingers hard and hushed me.

"Stop it, Carrie. You're embarrassing me," she'd said. Then she dipped her hand into her pocket, pulled out a tissue, and began to cry.

But this time, I didn't ask if anyone would wake. Instead, I stared at the school building and blocked out what was being said up front. I couldn't hear the squeal of children because school had closed for the occasion. The rest of the student body stood with me, crammed into the cemetery like sardines, huddling close to their families because one of our own was being put into the earth this time.

I stood between my parents and knew this funeral motorcade had been the biggest yet.

The ground under me felt soft. Even though it

was December, the earth definitely wasn't frozen yet because I sank down every time I switched weight from foot to foot. And every time I descended another inch, I had this fleeting sensation I was plummeting into the ground with my dead classmate.

The school's choir lit into "Amazing Grace." At the second verse, one girl stepped forward and sang a solo. And as I listened to Brenda Newell's clear, solid voice, I remembered the first time I realized everything around me was changing.

The wind whipped up, fluttering my skirt around my legs, and I lifted the collar of my coat over my chin. I hugged myself tight just like I had that night. It might've been only weeks before. But standing in the cemetery between my parents, it seemed like a century ago.

It'd been a cool October night, and rain the day before had made the game slippery and sloppy with mud. Football Homecoming showered down on my school with fortune and victory.

The Math Club had worked the concession stand. The cheerleaders had finished their celebration dance, flipping and twirling across the sidelines. The band was hyped from their full-throated rendition of "Peter Gunn." And I, editor of the school's journal, was cursed with the assignment of interviewing coach and quarterback after their conquest.

Popcorn and cups littered the still-lit, deserted stadium. The field was torn to shreds. One big puddle completely wiped out the fifty-yard line.

I leaned against the frosty brick wall of the gym and tried to shield myself from the October chill. But the cold sneaked in with every breath I took. It froze my lungs to my ribs and had me sucking in air through chattering teeth.

One geek in the Math Club had thought to be

funny and served me a diet soda when I'd ordered a regular. So there I was, nasty aftertaste clinging to my tongue, waiting for the jocks to arrive. I watched the line of red taillights as the parking lot cleared. A few people lingered, grouped by their cars, laughing and talking. My brother was among one of those crowds, waiting for me to finish my interview.

Marty didn't live at home anymore but he'd been going to the game anyway and had reluctantly let me ride with him. He'd graduated a couple of years before but since he was immature and had been a class clown, my generation still remembered and welcomed him into their clutches.

The opposing team shuffled onto their bus with their heads lowered. And here came the champs. Braying like a bunch of coon dogs, they looked pumped and riled. The ground rumbled under my feet as the stampede approached.

Still huddled together in one lumped mass, they came, charging toward the side door of the gym that led to their locker room. Cleats click-clacked on the asphalt parking lot, reminding me of my Great Aunt Kay's dog, Chigger, who liked to run across her linoleum floor, creating as much clatter as possible. The team blew by me, smelling of musty earth, sports cream and sweat.

I couldn't spot Coach Newell, but there *he* was, trailing at the end, grinning with the rest of the idiots: quarterback Luke Carter.

I rose onto my toes and waved my hand. "Luke," I called, and quickly dropped my fingers when I realized I probably looked like some overeager groupie.

The chanting was too loud, though. One player did glance my way, but moved on without speaking. All he saw of me was a long brown trench coat with a mop of fuzzy blond hair sticking out the top. Nothing worth pausing over, I'm sure.

"Carter!" I put a little more gut into the call and finally caught his attention.

In his red jersey smeared brown, he faltered a step, his head swiveling my way. Then with a quick sidestep, he slipped from the group and came toward me. The streetlights played the shadows like a puppeteer, dangling darkness over his torso and down. When he emerged from the shadows, I sucked in a breath. The football pads made his shoulders seem wider and his chest twice as broad, while thigh pads made his waistline look especially slim. He moved like he was full of cardboard, stiff and ambling.

He towered over me, a looming six feet two inches tall (according to the football roster) to my five feet seven. His helmet was off, hanging at his side, and he'd wrapped his fingers around the face guard. A cut across his right eyebrow sliced toward the corner of his eye. Tiny etches of blood filled the cracks and defined the spot where he'd have a healthy showing of crow's feet someday. His wet black hair curled slightly down his forehead and around his ears. And his eyes were a blue so clear that if they'd been a lake, I could've seen right to their rocky bottoms.

Finally, he smiled...and I wanted to kick him. He had a row of bright white teeth with a bit of an overbite, and a dimple I could've fallen into.

I hated him for that grin. I mean, how dare he look at me with those blue orbs and display such a genuine smile? I didn't want it. I didn't want to step into line behind every other girl in school whose heart went into double-thump for this boy. He had no right to give me that busted-ice feeling.

Yeah, busted ice. It's like making instant gelatin the fast way with ice instead of cold water. When the ice cubes drop into the boiling gelatin they crack and sometimes bust into a hundred pieces. Well, my stomach was full of a dozen of those cubes, busting and cracking all over inside me because Luke Carter was a vision.

"Yeah?" he asked, resting his helmet against his hip.

"Carrie Paxton," I said, sticking my hand in the space of air between us. I tried to keep it professional despite my irritation over the busted ice in my gut. "Editor of *The Central Record*."

"I know." He took my hand. Compared to his, my fingers were small and weak. "You're in my Trig class."

His handshake was cold and slightly damp. He squeezed my palm before letting go. My mouth dropped open.

He wasn't supposed to know that about me.

I'm sorry. But no girl, despite how much that girl doesn't care about popularity and all that junk, can remain calm when someone like Luke Carter shakes her hand and actually knows her name. OK, I admit he should've known my name. We'd gone to the same school since kindergarten. But noticing me enough to realize we shared a class? No way.

"Oh," I said. If I'd had any air left in my lungs, I might've been able to continue, but I did a fairly decent job of making a fool out of myself as it was. "Well. I...I...I mean, is it OK to talk to you, er, ask you a few questions about the game? For the paper, that is."

"Sure." A bead of muddy sweat trickled out of his hairline and down his temple, mixing with blood before moving on. Fascinated, I watched it drool a crooked path down his cheek and neck and then into the collar of his jersey.

As if catching my entranced stare, he lifted the hand that held his helmet and wiped the sweat away with the back of his palm. "What do you want to know?"

I cleared my throat and dropped my eyes. "Umm, well..." I yanked a notebook from the inside pocket of my trench coat. The wind caught a few sheets, making the lined pages flail and thrash like they were drowning in the ocean or something. I tried to get a hold of them and rein them in but only succeeded in wrinkling most of the pad.

"Sorry," I muttered, and dug deep into my outer pocket, frantically searching for my pen. I couldn't find the irritating thing there, and switched hands on the notebook to search the other pocket. I didn't dare look up. I could feel *him* watching and it made my cheeks hot.

He coughed, trying to get my attention, and my head flew up—long bangs falling into my eyes. He motioned toward my right ear with his index finger. I frowned, wondering if there was a twig or something in my hair and reached up, patting the area. And the pen, which had been securely tucked behind my ear, stabbed me.

"Ouch!" I yanked the pen out of my hair and set it firmly to the flapping paper.

"You OK?" he asked. I could see the amused crinkling at the corners of his eyes where he tried not to laugh at me.

I sniffed, more fueled with anger at his mockery than with embarrassment. "So Mr. Carter," I started. What could I say to really upset him? I tossed my head to get the hair out of my eyes. "How does it feel to be Stillburrow's poster child?"

His eyebrows drew together and his forehead wrinkled. He was just as appealing frowning as he was smiling. I swallowed, and more busted ice crackled in my guts.

"I wouldn't say I was Stillburrow's poster child. I wouldn't say that at all."

I lifted one eyebrow as if to disagree, when, well...OK, I totally disagreed. "But you're the one everyone cheers for."

To this day, I don't know what possessed me to be so rude to him. My blood was still pumping to the wrong parts of my body, bypassing the pathway to my brain, I guess. If only he had some flaws. Then maybe I would've let up. But the impact he had on me felt so alarming my "fight or flight" instincts kicked in. So I fought the feeling. Frantically.

"It's *your* name written on all the posters on Main Street, and you're the one who's mentioned in the headline of every football article. It's you who—"

"Hey, you're the editor of said paper, not me." He took a step toward me, pointing a finger at my chest, looming even taller. "If you don't want me in every article then you should—"

"I don't usually write the sports section," I said through gritted teeth. "And as I was saying before you interrupted, this town's never paid so much attention to football until this year. It all adds up. You're the quarterback, the team captain. And tonight we beat Valley, which we haven't done since 1996."

"It wasn't one against eleven out there tonight. It was *eleven* against eleven. We all played our hearts out. I couldn't have done anything without my teammates. They," he paused to jab his finger toward the locker room door, "are the ones who made me look good, not the other way around. I don't like how you're making me out to be so self-centered. We played like a team, won like a team, and I was just a part of that. It wasn't me. It was everyone. And I'm proud of every guy that stepped onto the field. We deserved that win." He was shouting by the time he'd finished.

His lips trembled, and I wondered what they'd feel like. Right then, they'd be hot and moist and passionate. My breath caught, and I made myself calm down, made myself think logically. I took a step back. I'd never kissed anyone before or been kissed. And whatever force had caused me to dream about a little lip action right then, and with Luke Carter at that, really freaked me out.

I glanced down at the notebook and realized I'd copied what he'd said.

"Is that your official quote?" I asked after a long, steadying breath.

He shook his head as if to clear it. "What?"

"That was a good speech, Carter." I tried to ignore the persistent thump in my chest. "Can I put it in the paper?"

He didn't answer, and when I risked looking up, he stared at me with his mouth opened in a surprised O. He stood so close I could feel his heat. He smelled musky, like he'd soaked in the scent of the air right before a warm summer rain. I wanted to run away. And I wanted to move closer.

"Hey, Carter! Great game."

We both jumped and spun toward Coach Newell as he jogged over and slapped a hand to Luke's back. "Best moves I've seen on the field since I started coaching." He looked at me. "Dean Paxton's girl, right?" His voice had an echoing boom to it.

"Yes, sir." I stood up, straightening my back, thinking this barrel-chested man could be a great drill sergeant.

"Doing an article for the paper?" he asked. I nodded. "Well, I've got a load of quotes for you tonight."

Even his smile seemed to roar. He started in, his voice thundering with each statement. I jotted down sentences madly, trying to keep up, but not listening to a word he said. Luke left in the middle of it, escaping inside the gym. I felt an odd mixture of panic and release as he faded off.

When Coach Newell finished, he asked if I had enough for an article. I said I had enough for a novel and he hooted, throwing back his head to let out a resounding laugh. Obviously, he liked the sound of that and asked if he'd get his picture on the cover. I don't remember how I responded but it caused him to chortle again. Then he pummeled me on the back with the palm of his hand, knocking me off balance, and sent me on my way.

With pages full of quotes, I searched for Marty. My shaking hands cramped from gripping my notebook too tight.

"Way to go, Carrie," I muttered to myself, forgetting Coach Newell and thinking only of the almost-interview before that. "Get a crush on the best looking, most popular, rich boy in school. How original."

When I caught sight of my brother, I pulled up short. Marty stood amidst a group of people, but it wasn't his normal group. He usually hung out with other class-clown types, goof-offs and dropouts. But this night, he was surrounded by a bunch of cheerleaders. And the main focus of his attention was Abby Eggrow. He'd been working at Getty's General for a few months as the bagger and Abby Eggrow just so happened to be the cashier there. I knew he'd been interested in her, but seeing them together with my own eyes was something else altogether.

I had no idea what was going on in his mind. Why was he putting the moves on *her* of all people? Abby was one of the privileged elite who had money and a future. She was five years younger than Marty, a year older than me, and everyone in town knew her plans. Next year she was going off to college to become a doctor. Marty's big plans involved saving most of his weekly earnings to party with his friends on the weekend.

Yes, what a pair they made. Seeing Abby smile up at my brother was like seeing a full carat diamond set in a plastic ring from a Cracker Jack box. It was like seeing me hooked up with Luke Carter.

I clutched my notebook to my chest and waited until Marty glanced over and saw me. When he did, his smile faded a little. He reached for Abby's elbow and bent over her as he spoke. From where I stood, I couldn't tell exactly what happened next. But Abby rose on her toes and either whispered something in his ear or kissed him on the cheek. Either way, Marty ogled her like a lovesick idiot when she pulled away. Then he bowed his head and turned toward me.

I couldn't blame him too much, though. I mean, hadn't I just done basically the same thing? I'd spent the last twenty minutes gawking at Luke Carter. Of course, unlike Marty, I knew I had no chance with Luke.

"Done with your little interview already?" he asked, striding past me and hopping into the cab of his truck. He started the engine as I climbed into the passenger side.

"Yes," I said, and slammed the door. "Are you finished flirting with all the cheerleaders yet?" I glanced over and smirked when he frowned.

"Did Carter dazzle you with a bunch of cute quotes?" he shot back.

Refusing to rise to his bait, I faced forward and crossed my arms over my chest. "Don't forget you're taking me into Paulbrook tomorrow so I can turn in next week's paper to get printed."

Marty snickered, probably thinking he'd just scored a major point, and shifted the car into drive. I had to hold onto the door's armrest for dear life as he roared out of the parking spot.

"I've got to work tomorrow," he answered, and lifted a few fingers to wave at the cheerleaders we passed.

Linda Kage

I rolled my eyes when a few waved back. "Well, when do you get out?"

He sighed. "Two."

"Then pick me up at two thirty."

"I'm not your chauffeur."

"I know. It's worse. You're my brother."

"At least you ended up with a cool brother. Look what I got for a sister."

Sending him an arch look, I sweetly said, "Give me a ride tomorrow or I'm telling Mom about that time you broke her—"

"OK, OK," he broke in a little too quickly. "Geez, brat, you win. I'll give you a lift. Just shut up already."

We rode home in silence until Marty pulled to the curb in front of our family home. He left the engine running, waiting for me to get out.

I paused. "Coming in to say hi?"

He shifted on the vinyl seat like it had suddenly become too uncomfortable to sit on.

"No."

I lifted my eyebrows in mock surprise. "Why not?"

He glared. "I wouldn't want to get mud on the carpet with my dirty shoes."

I shrugged like it didn't matter what he did, and opened the door. "Well, Mom wants to see you."

When Marty snorted out a dry laugh, I turned quickly to stare at him. His head fell back and rested on the back of the bench seat. My heart broke a little when he said, "Mom doesn't know what she wants."

Chapter Two

Our town, Stillburrow, is surrounded by Kansas wheat fields. With a population of just under seven hundred and decreasing, it's the type of town where anyone living here was born here. People don't move to Stillburrow. They move out.

A throwback to the fifties, it still has a Mom and Pop Store called Getty's General, run by John Getty himself, whose granddad started the place back in 1944. Across the street, his brother Fredrick runs Fred's Diner. Both of these establishments sit on Main Street, which is the only paved street in town and stretches a total of six blocks long.

Geographically, Stillburrow is built in a simple layout. It's located in the flattest part of Kansas, thirty miles north of Paulbrook (what we called *the city*—Paulbrook has a university, a hospital, an amusement park and everything else Stillburrow doesn't). North of Paulbrook on Highway 23, there's a turn off heading east, called Still Road. That's our road.

After three miles as Still Road, its name changes to Main Street—the official "city limits" of Stillburrow begin—and the gravel roadway becomes asphalt. On the main drag, there's the gas station, then Getty's General Store and Fred's. Georgia's Barber Shop, The First State Bank and one of our four churches are all located on the next block. We also have the funeral home, dentist office, post office and City Hall on Main Street. At the other end of town, where the city limit ends and Still Road starts up again, pavement changes back into gravel. There we have a bar and grill across from the city pool, before wheat fields crop up once more as if nothing had disturbed their space.

All the streets running east and west, except for Main, are named after trees. There's Oak, Pine, Birch, Walnut and Elm. Running north and south, the streets are named after presidents. The president streets are in historical order, starting at the west end of town with Washington and ending at the east with Jackson.

I live on the northeast edge of Stillburrow, right across from the park on the corner of Oak and Jackson. Jackson Street's a weird road because when it crosses Main, it curves around until it intersects with Quincy and becomes Birch. But that works out well for me because the school's on Birch and it makes my walk to class easier.

Almost everything's on Main Street, except for a few biggies. We have three churches not on Main as well as the park (which is deserted ten months of the year), the library, Dean's Auto Shop—that also serves as a used car lot—and the school.

The school's the heart of the town.

Stillburrow focuses its attention on its children. Stillburrow Education Center, also known as SEC, holds classes from kindergarten through twelfth grade. The grade school is on the east end of the building and the high school is on the west. Years ago, the city built a sports complex, with a track, football field, gymnasium, and ball diamond for the school. It's not next to the school building but is located just outside town on Still Road. Most towns have a sign introducing their city with a population number under it. But not us. We have the SEC Sports Complex with its manicured lawns and impressive, lighted stadium.

Like I said, Stillburrow prides itself on its younger generation.

But we don't start our education at SEC. Mrs. Eggrow, the principal's wife, runs the preschool across the street from SEC in a yellow two-story house, where many children learn to read and write before they walk. Actually, all the parents in town seemed to be in one big competition to see who'd end up with the brightest kid.

Mrs. Wallace was sure her daughter, Theresa, would become a famous actress. Theresa was a senior when I was in third grade. I can still remember how she glowed on stage. That was the year the drama club had six plays and sold out every seat in the auditorium each production. And Theresa did get pretty far. She made it all the way to Hollywood before she fell in with the wrong group of people and died on an acid trip. I remember how school was let out that day, as well, and everyone in town attended the funeral. Up until this year, she was our big tragedy.

After Theresa's death, the competition over star children died off for a while. Most kids graduated and stuck around Stillburrow, or went off to Paulbrook.

Then a couple of years ago it all started again. It seemed a few kids around town showed special talent in their field of expertise. There was Timmy Newell, the football coach's son, who could play the trumpet like he was a member of the New York Symphony. His twin sister, Brenda, had a singing voice that could make you cry to hear. Coach Newell was a little put off when his kids turned out to be more musical than athletic but that didn't stop his thick chest from swelling each time someone complimented him for his children's abilities.

Rick Getty—who was going steady with Brenda—could paint like Andrew Wyeth. Jill

Anderson, the late Theresa Wallace's niece, tried her hand at acting though she wasn't as talented as her aunt had been. And Luke Carter was the best quarterback the town had ever seen. His dad was president of the bank and most town folk had their hopes set high on Luke.

Mom tried to talk me up for being the editor of *The Central Record*. It was only the school's paper, but since the town didn't have a newspaper of its own, everyone subscribed to *The Central Record* and read it like it was the town paper. Mom thought I'd make it big someday with my writing. And that was my dream too, to be a star investigative reporter in some big city, becoming nationally famous. But I was only the town mechanic's girl and not too widely known.

I didn't mind who I was. I was proud of my father. He was honest and owned his own business, which was impressive in my eyes. I didn't care if the mortgage on the house was maxed out or if the bank owned over half his shop. Most people still looked down on my parents because they had married right before my mom graduated from high school, when she found out she was pregnant with Marty. But that's a small town for you. People give out their gossip and their snooty opinions like they're the Word of God.

Once upon a time, I thought such prejudices against people were so old fashioned they no longer existed, but then I grew old enough to hear and understand more. And yes, they're still around. They are in Stillburrow, anyhow.

Mom tried to overcome the "scandal" by being the perfect housewife, like she could scrub away her past. So I grew up in a clean home. Well, OK, maybe clean is too mild a word for it. Sterile would fit better. I didn't know what dirt was until I was five and asked my dad what all that brown stuff was in the grass outside. Mom also thought if she attended every PTO meeting, if she had her hair done every week at Georgia Anderson's Hair Salon, or if she volunteered to bring food to every potluck dinner, she'd be accepted. But she claimed people still talked behind her back.

Dad just shrugged her worries off, doing and saying exactly what he would've done anyway. People still gave him their business but when they walked away from his shop, Mom said they would shake their heads and whisper, "It's a shame what he and that pretty little Andrea Burke (that's my mom) did back when she was a senior in high school."

Dad was a hard-working man and I helped him sometimes in his shop. I'd only started doing this recently, though. Marty used to be his right-hand man. But since the parents in town had started back into the competitive spirit, Mom had been putting pressure on Marty, and they'd had a falling out a few months before. So after a pretty loud yelling match between my mother and brother, Marty moved out and was currently living in an old rundown shack with his friend, Austin Fitz.

Like I've already mentioned, Marty started working at Getty's General. Dad gave him a hard time for being a grocery store clerk at twenty-three. But I don't think it was Marty's life ambition to become one. It just turned out that way. Both Mom and Dad thought he could be so much more. I, on the other hand, had my doubts.

Since he'd been gone, I'd spent some time standing around the shop while Dad crawled under cars. I handed him screwdrivers and stuff. Piece by piece, I was learning what a carburetor and a head gasket were. And if I felt so inclined, I could even change the oil in a car or switch out a flat tire. Dad started calling me his little mechanic. Mom made me shower every time I stepped foot inside the house after helping him.

I was helping Dad one Saturday afternoon, a little over a week after Football Homecoming and that dreaded interview, when Luke Carter strolled into the car lot next to the shop. Mom was gone uptown to get her hair styled and I was thumbing through one of Dad's magazines, leaning against the workbench and looking at pictures of old cars, when I saw the movement out of the corner of my eye.

I looked up and the paralysis set in. Dad was asking me for a nine-sixteenths wrench. But his voice sounded distant and its meaning didn't set in.

Then Dad noticed Luke too—or noticed me noticing him. And he slid out from under the engine. He dusted off his pants, pulled a cleaning rag from his back pocket and wiped his hands. Walking out toward Luke, he called a greeting and I felt compelled to follow. The gravel crunched under our shoes as we neared Luke, who was slowly circling a black '93 Ford Mustang like some kind of prospective buyer.

He looked wonderful. His shoes were leather Dockers. His designer jeans were held snug around his waist by a thin, black leather belt, and he wore his letterman's jacket, bright red with the school emblem of a brave weighted down with medals, over a navy blue collared shirt. He wore a lot of blue, which was good, since I thought he looked best in that color. The top two buttons of his shirt were undone, and he had the shadow of a beard along his jaw as if he hadn't shaved in a while. It gave him that masculine, rugged appeal and made him look too mature for a mere seventeen.

"Car shopping?" Dad asked, stuffing the rag back in his pocket and crossing his arms over his chest. He planted his feet wide. He always stood that way when he got into talking cars with someone. It was like he was in a boat, braced for anyone trying to rock him with the wave of an unsolvable automobile problem.

"Maybe," Luke said. "Since I'm going to college next year, I'll need a car. And Dad's making me buy my own. He thinks it'll teach me to watch my finances. So..." He rubbed the back of his neck and sent a quick glance my way, making my stomach churn with nervous jitters.

He turned his attention back to Dad and I lifted my hand to my mouth to chew on the nail of my index finger.

"I was just checking out my options," Luke said with a shrug.

Dad stood by him and stared at the Mustang. He rubbed his chin thoughtfully and then glanced at Luke. "You going to Paulbrook University, then?"

"Yes, sir." Luke darted another look at me.

"Are you going to be staying at home when you go to college, or will you find some place in the city?"

I wanted to tell my dad to quit interrogating him. Instead, I shifted my weight from one leg to the other and crossed my arms over my chest. I stared at the gravel between my feet and soaked in every word Luke said.

"I was planning on staying home. At least through my first year."

"Well," Dad drawled the word slowly. "Commuting to the city everyday's going to be a long drive." He glanced toward the Mustang. "And this thing here is quite the gas guzzler."

Luke made a noise of understanding. "I guess it wouldn't be very practical then."

Dad nodded. "Now if you want something that's got good mileage..." He turned from the sporty coupe. "This Toyota will run forever on a single tank."

Three pair of eyes moved to the blue compact

car. I almost slapped my hand to my forehead and groaned. The car was so un-Luke-Carter-like, I felt embarrassed for...well, for all three of us. Luke for meeting someone who actually assumed he'd ever drive this heap, my dad for misreading his customer so badly, and me for witnessing the mortifying exchange.

Besides the dent in the back door on the driver's side, the Toyota's previous owner had been Loma Myers. And the only reason her daughter had confiscated the keys and sold it was because Loma was being put into a nursing home and was too senile to drive anymore. I couldn't believe my dad even considered selling the old hunk of scrap metal to Luke.

Dad must've realized his mistake or he read the look of complete horror on Luke's face because he went on, scratching his chin again. "We don't have a lot of options here." We only had about seven or eight cars on the lot. "But if you think up any questions or see anything you're interested in, I'll be in the shop there."

"OK," Luke said. "Sure thing."

Dad nodded and started back toward the garage. His mind, I knew, had already returned to his work. I pivoted to follow him when Luke spoke.

"Hi, Carrie."

I stopped and pressed a hand against the constriction in my chest before I could face him. Then I dropped my fingers to my sides and turned back. "Hi."

"I read your article about the game." He left the Mustang and neared me. "Good piece."

"Thank you." The words came out a hoarse, garbled mess because my throat had dried up, and I had to clear it. "Thanks," I repeated.

"The only thing is..." He slowly began to circle me as he had the Mustang. "I don't ever go by the

20

name Lucas." He looked up and stopped. I fell into a trance staring back at those hypnotic blues, and I couldn't glance away.

I swallowed. He'd caught my barb. Everyone knew how much Luke detested his Christian name. And that's exactly why I'd called him Lucas Carter in the article.

He started walking again, kicking a little at the gravel. "I figure there's really only four times in my life I have to suffer through it. The day I was born since it's on my birth certificate, the day I graduate, the day I get married, and the day of my funeral. So unless you're planning on killing me off or marrying me, I'd really appreciate it if you'd just call me Luke." He looked up again for my response.

I could only nod.

He lifted one of his eyebrows. "You already knew that though, didn't you? That I hate my name?"

My voice sounded small when I answered. "Yes."

"Then why'd you do it?"

I shrugged. "I don't know." *Maybe because I don't want anyone to know I like you.*

He gave a small laugh and looked off across the street toward the park. It was empty except for a few squirrels chasing each other. No one bothered with the metal playground equipment when the weather turned cold.

"You know," he said, and rubbed the back of his neck again. I bit down on my fingernail. "You're not like any girl I've ever met before."

I wasn't sure if that was a compliment or a complaint so I decided not to answer.

"Do you…" He stopped rubbing his neck. I guess he realized he'd been revealing a nervous habit because he stuffed his hands in his pockets. My mind whirled. Luke Carter was acting nervous? Around me?! I was beginning to get the feeling he hadn't stopped by just to look at cars.

Stop trying to give yourself an ego boost, Carrie. What would Luke Carter want with a skinny, stick girl like you? I mean, look at you. Stained jeans, an old bulky sweater you stole from your brother's closet, the picture of the brave half worn off the front. And that hair, slopped up in a quick ponytail. Not to mention everyone in school thinks you're the oddest, most reclusive person to walk the halls.

I let out a deflated breath.

Luke had been looking off across the street at the park, but suddenly he turned back. "Do you want to walk in the park?"

A walk? Beside Luke Carter? I darted a look around me. He couldn't be talking to me. But Dad was busy, whistling in the shop. And Mom wasn't due home for a while, not with the town's gossip, Georgia Anderson, styling her hair. The rest of the houses around looked bored and lifeless. I glanced back up at him and almost jumped. He was staring directly at me. He definitely wasn't talking to anyone else.

I was about to decline, say I should be helping Dad, when Luke took my hand and grabbed the opportunity away from me. I could've pulled away. But with my palm sheathed in his warm, protective fingers, I would've followed him anywhere just then.

"So you like to write, huh?" he asked as we crossed the street. Stillburrow Park wasn't large, and since the swing set and the jungle gym were the only pieces of equipment in the recreation area, we were pretty much forced to head toward them. They stood under a couple of large sycamore trees.

"I guess," I said. And then, being a little nervous—OK, being very nervous—I started rambling. Out came details of my dream to be an investigative reporter. Out came my plans to apply for a scholarship the next year and then eventually work my way through college. Yes, I blabbed it all to him.

And he listened. I could tell he really listened too, because he kept interrupting and asking questions. He asked what kind of things I wrote and how often. It was so disconcerting to think he would even care. But he talked to me in a way that eased my whacked out nerves, and I began to grow comfortable being there with him. I mean, well, I got as comfortable as I could with my heart rate going overtime and my hands turning into quivering balls of nerves. It was like the happy medium between utter euphoria and a complete panic attack.

At the swings, he sat me down. It was the oddest thing. But it felt so natural. My fingers wrapped around the cold metal chains and he pushed me slowly back and forth. I lifted my face into the biting wind and smiled. This couldn't be real. Luke Carter was pushing me on the swings.

I stared up at the tree limbs above me.

"There's still one green leaf left on the tree," I said, thinking that it was somehow significant, like some kind of sign for hope.

"Fair youth, beneath the trees, thou canst not leave / Thy song, nor ever can those trees be bare," Luke said.

His voice didn't echo but the words seemed to dangle in the air over us, leaving a presence that filled my chest with a heavy yearning. The single leaf above me rippled in the breeze and I shivered. I thought I could gladly be frozen there for eternity, stuck like that, listening to the twitter of birds and the squeak of the swing's rusty hinges. I could inhale the brisk fragrance of autumn and absorb the sweet embrace of romance forever.

"John Keats wrote that."

I glanced up at Luke and caught the distinct outline of his face in profile. Maybe I'd never seen his side view before, or only looked at him from the front, but he didn't look at all like the suave Luke Carter he usually was. His eyelashes were lowered as he squinted up at the sun. And his overbite was so pronounced it was the only thing I could focus on. He'd probably been a thumb sucker when he was a baby and it'd made his teeth jut out like that.

It caught me completely off guard. I'd never seen him from this angle and it made him appear somewhat insecure and lost. He stared up at the sky like it was a map that might tell him where he was and where he should go next.

But then he glanced down at me, and he was once again Luke Carter, football star and Stillburrow's poster child. I had this urge to tell him to turn back like he'd been a moment before because, for some reason, I liked him better with the malformed teeth and helpless expression.

"What?" he said, frowning at the odd look I was giving him.

I cleared my throat and glanced away. "The poem," I said. "It's pretty,"

"It's sad. Keats was only twenty-four years old and he knew he was dying when he wrote it."

I thought about that. Twenty-four felt so far away. But for dying, it was way too close.

"A finished body full of unfinished thoughts," Luke murmured. He pushed the swing again. I rocked forward. "I came up with that on my own."

I smiled and closed my eyes when his hands touched my back again to push. "A finished body full of unfinished thoughts," I repeated on a murmur. "I like that. You should write it down."

"Yeah. Maybe." The sound of his voice caused me to open my eyes. He sounded...I don't know. Wistful, I guess.

I was going to ask him about it but the moment was taken away from us. A car passed by on the street. I glanced over and saw the cheerleaders.

Liz Curry and Jill Anderson were creeping by, staring at us through the windshield of Liz's car. I stood up. And that's when Luke moved in front of me, completely blocking me from their view. He did it so subtly that if I hadn't been tuned into every movement he made, I wouldn't have noticed. The girls hollered a hello out their windows to him and he waved back, calling his own greeting.

I could already see the chain of gossip burning like a fuse to dynamite right through the town. Jill Anderson would tell her mother, who was fixing my mom's hair even as we stood there. I would hear about it at supper. Mom would play twenty questions with me. *What were you doing with that nice Carter boy? Does he have a date for the prom yet? Did he ask you out?*

Except there would be no gossip because the girls hadn't seen me. Luke had made sure of it.

"What's wrong?" Luke said.

I looked up and swallowed. "Nothing."

His return look implied he didn't believe me, but he let it go. "OK," he answered. "Well anyway. I was wondering…"

We were a few feet apart now and the intimacy from a moment ago had totally vanished. He went back to rubbing his neck.

"Did you just step in front of me so they couldn't see who you were with?" I blurted out.

His head snapped up. His eyes were wide and bright. "What?"

For the briefest of moments, I had been on top of the world. I'd actually thought he was going to ask me out, maybe even invite me to go to the lake party with him. The lake party was a student-organized event and reportedly very wild. It happened every year, contrary to what parents believed. And I'd truly thought I, Carrie Paxton, daughter to the town grease monkey, would show up at the school's biggest bash of the year on the arm of none other than Luke Carter himself. I'd even imagined how everyone would pause and say hi to us. How when it turned cold, he'd slide his letterman's jacket over my shoulders. And when it grew dark, we'd slip from the group and walk alone through the woods or along the edge of the lake.

I could almost hear the gossip that would follow us. Who does she think she is, trying to cuddle up to him? There's only one thing he'd want from her.

I frowned. He could have any girl in school. Heck, two of them had driven by moments before, waving and yelling. I don't know what I'd been thinking, but he'd certainly set me straight with that blocking move. It didn't lessen the sting, though.

"Why'd you do that?" I asked, setting my hands on my hips and giving him a glare I usually reserved for Marty.

"What're you talking about?" Suddenly, he was all innocence and confusion.

"You didn't want Liz and Jill to see me here with you," I said. "You stepped in front of me so they couldn't."

He laughed then, a nervous sound. "I did not."

"Why?" I said again, this time through gritted teeth. I wasn't about to let him get away with hurting me. I didn't care how big my crush for him was.

He blushed then, and kicked at a clump of dead leaves on the ground. "I don't know why you think I tried to block...Oh, never mind."

He said this to the leaves and jammed his hands into his pockets. When he looked up, he had to squint because the sun flickered through the tree branches, momentarily blinding him. A sliver of light briefly glowed golden over him, giving him unattainable, angelic appeal.

"No need to explain," I said. "I already know

why, anyway."

He stared at me hard. "You do?"

"You're embarrassed to be seen with me because you're so much better than I am." At his startled, appalled expression, I began to feel bolder. "You're the bank president's son and I'm just a mechanic's daughter. Isn't that why?"

His mouth fell open. "But that's the stupidest thing I've ever heard."

"It's not to me." I stomped my foot and scared a squirrel into darting up a tree. I wanted to cry. "You're a real snob, you know that?"

"Snob?!" For a second he didn't move. I saw the brief flash of pain in the clenching of his jaw before his brooding eyebrows huddled down protectively low over his eyes.

Then he snorted out a disbelieving laugh. Sucking his mouth around his overbite, he buried his hands in his hair and clutched his head. "I can't believe I'm hearing this."

For a moment he was quiet, and then he laughed out another snort. But this time it was a harsher, more cynical sound. "This is crazy, Carrie. You don't make any sense. Why would I invite you to walk in the park and then not want to be seen with you?"

"I don't know," I whispered. "Why did you?" My teeth dug into my bottom lip and I could feel moisture gathering at the corners of my eyes. My chin trembled.

He opened his mouth but closed it again. "I'm sorry," he finally said, furiously rubbing that spot on the back of his neck. "I just had an idea. A *bad* idea, I guess." And he walked away, calling over his shoulder, "I've got to go."

My breath caught in my throat as I watched him retreat. A voice inside me shrieked, "Go after him, Carrie. Call out, 'Luke! What's your idea?'"

But I did nothing. Numbed and a little shell-shocked, I watched him walk away until he disappeared around a house at the end of the block.

Then I ran home, locked myself in my room and didn't come out until supper.

Chapter Three

The next day right after lunch, I walked into Getty's General with a shopping list and a letter gripped in my hand. During church, Pastor Curry had talked about the sins of the father. There was an empty spot in the pew next to me and every time the door would open, admitting a latecomer, Mom would peer around me to get a look at who entered. But Marty never showed. So there I was, standing in the general store with Mom's hastily thought-up list and a note for my brother.

I couldn't get you-know-who out of my head. So when Mom commissioned me to go pseudo-grocery shopping for her, I was more than ready for the distraction. Luke didn't attend the same church we did. He went to the chapel on Main Street. So I didn't have to worry about getting stuck staring at the back of his head during the service or anything. But that didn't stop me from thinking about him.

By this time, I had come up with a plausible reason why he had visited me the day before. It must've been because of what I'd called him in the paper. He didn't want to be referred to as Lucas, so he'd come to my house and made sure I wouldn't do it again. That had to be the reason, right?

But that didn't explain why he'd asked me to walk in the park with him. We'd discussed the whole Lucas bit before he'd asked for that stroll. So why had he asked? I was back at the beginning again. Biting my lip, I thought about it harder.

And then the explanation finally came to me. He'd been buttering me up. Luke probably thought if he was extra nice to me, if he took a walk with me and fluttered his pretty-boy lashes a few times, I'd be less likely to call him Lucas again. And it'd worked. I'd slipped right into his clever scheme—for a minute there anyway.

But Jill and Liz driving by had ruined his strategy. If he'd been caught in the park with me, his reputation would've taken a severe nosedive. He had no choice but to move quickly and dodge in front of me. He'd succeeded in blocking me out of the way. No one knew I'd been there with him. But now *I* was onto his game. If only I were stupid, he could've had me in complete adoration of him by now, right where he wanted me, and thus I would never bad-mouth him in *The Central Record* again.

It was a low blow for me, but very clever of him. Too bad I was smarter. And too bad I still felt butterflies in my stomach every time I thought of him. I wish I could've hated him completely and been done with it. Instead, I felt betrayed and hurt.

I unfolded Mom's list and read the contents: milk, eggs, and flour. It wasn't too original, so I slipped a pen out of my pocket and scrawled in chocolate almond ice cream at the bottom.

Hey, if I was being forced to do her dirty work, I might as well get paid for it.

The store was fairly dead. It was open only from noon to five on Sundays and that was for just-in-case items, like someone needing extra potatoes for their Sunday dinner. The sheriff's wife, Mrs. Bates, was shopping as I started up the produce aisle to get to the milk and the eggs in the back.

The store was small, only four rows wide, so I had my list completed within the minute. Marty was at the checkout line talking to Abby Eggrow. She'd been working there about as long as he had and was showing up to school in a lot of new outfits since she'd started.

She smiled up at my brother, blushed and tucked a straight lock of hair behind her ear. Marty was half sitting on the end of the conveyer belt with one foot still on the tiled floor and one folded under him. He had a Blow Pop stick poking out of his mouth and there was a bulge in his cheek where the sucker was stashed.

He was tall and skinny as all get out, with a thirty-eight inch inseam to his Wrangler jeans. He had the same pale blond hair I did. But his neck was longer and his Adam's apple jutted out noticeably. I suppose if I wasn't his sister and didn't know he was an idiot, I might say he was attractive. Lots of girls said he looked like Leonardo DiCaprio. I thought that was stretching it. But sometimes when he wasn't bugging me, he didn't look too bad.

When he saw me he didn't stand, he just transferred the lollypop from one side of his cheek to the other.

"Hey, brat."

Abby's head spun around and her face went beet red, as if she'd been caught in the back seat of a car with him over at the camping ground—which was the major make-out spot for all Stillburrow teenagers.

"Hi, Carrie," she said.

If I kept a notebook of firsts, I'd have to scribble down her "Hi, Carrie," as the first time Abby Eggrow ever voluntarily spoke to me.

"Ready for the big test in history tomorrow?" she asked.

Another first. Abby smiling and asking me a question, instead of treating me like I was invisible. I wondered if the apocalypse had begun.

For the sake of my brother, I pushed all rude thoughts out of my brain and nodded politely to her.

I told her, in my most respectful tone, that I wasn't ready for the test at all. History with Mr. Decker was not my strong point. Neither was trigonometry for that matter. But Abby always seemed to know what questions would be on all the history tests. So on a crazy whim, I invited her to come over after supper and maybe help me study.

I never asked people to my house. And Abby Eggrow wouldn't have been my first choice. But asking her over would be like inviting Marty as well. And a little discomfort at having a guest would surely be overridden by my duty to my parents in coercing Marty to come and visit them.

Or maybe I just liked to stir the pot.

"Oh...uh, sorry, but I can't," she said, not sounding sorry at all. "I'm going to the movies in Paulbrook tonight. But I've heard Mr. Decker asks a lot of questions about Appomattox Court House."

I had no idea what the Appomattox Court House was and made a mental note to find out.

Abby ran me through the checkout line and I paid with the bill Mom had given me. Then Mrs. Bates, by the cleaning supplies, called for help. As Abby glided off to assist the sheriff's wife, I turned to Marty and watched him double bag the ice cream.

"Got a letter for you," I said. He stopped bagging and glanced up. "From Mom," I added and slid the envelope down the conveyer belt to him. His shoulders deflated a little but he grabbed it up and pulled out the letter as well as a twenty-dollar bill. He jammed the money into his pocket with one hand and unfolded the note with his other.

His eyebrows instantly rose. "Walking in the park with Luke Carter, huh?"

I clenched my teeth and folded my arms over my chest, refusing to show any embarrassment or shock. Mom hadn't said anything to me last night. She hadn't even let on that she'd known at all.

Dad must've told her.

I tried to ignore the heat rising to my face and shrugged with one lazy shoulder. "I wrote an article about Homecoming for the paper, featuring the coach and quarterback." Then I got angry with myself, wondering why I was trying to explain it to Marty.

"Uh-huh. I read it." He snorted the name *Lucas* under his breath and went back to reading Mom's note. "And helping out the old man in the shop too? You've been a busy girl, brat."

"I wouldn't have to help him if you'd come home," I said between my teeth, since I couldn't seem to get them unclenched.

He glanced up once with a quick scowl, then back down and finished the letter. "And tell Mom I can't make it for supper." He shot a quick glance toward Abby. When he looked back at me, he was stuffing the letter into his back pocket. He wiggled his eyebrows. "I'm going to the movies tonight."

My arms unfolded and my hands ground into my hips. "Just what do you think you're doing?" He frowned and I stepped closer, lowering my voice. "She's only eighteen."

"Only?" He laughed and tugged on my hair. "That's over a year older than you."

"And five years too young for you!"

He pulled back. "So what? Dad's seven years older than Mom."

My mouth fell open. "It's that serious, then? You're thinking marriage?"

"No!" He backed away from the counter and ripped the lollypop out of his mouth. "It's just a date. Nothing serious."

"Then why're you fooling around with her in the first place?" I said, lowering my voice even more. "She's leaving in a year to get a *real* life. What do you have to offer her, Marty? A stock boy's salary? It looks pretty worthless to me. I mean, the whole relationship is going nowhere right from the beginning."

He scoffed and pointed the lollypop at my head. "Well, aren't you the pot calling the kettle black? Or have you already forgotten about your little stroll with Luke Carter?"

My jaw felt tight. I took a second to gather my thoughts. OK, I was just trying to cool my temper because I wanted to hit him—bad. If he hadn't mentioned Luke, I might've been able to sniff and walk off. But since I was still sore about Mr. Carter, I had to strike back. When I felt clear I spoke, my voice cool.

"Excuse me," I said, "but I am not, nor will I ever, go to the movies with Luke Carter. I'm not stupid like you. The only reason he came to see me yesterday was to yell at me for putting his full name in the paper."

Marty wasn't buying it, though. "He had to hold your hand for that?" he taunted.

If there were ever a moment I could've killed my parents, that would've been it. I felt my face flame red. Dad must've watched the entire episode of Luke and me in the park. But would he have mentioned the hand-holding part to Mom? And would Mom have put it in her letter to Marty? I seriously doubted it, so I took my chances and called his bluff.

"He did not," I said with force. "Mom didn't put that in your letter. You made it up."

I knew he'd made it up when he leaned over the counter and snickered. "I bet you wanted him to, though."

"No, not at all," I announced, primly raising my chin a notch as if to say I considered myself too good for the likes of Luke Carter. *I'm* too smart to fall for a pretty face." I glanced over to where Abby was still chatting with Mrs. Bates. "Tell me, Marty. Is she as enlightening to talk to as she is to stare at? Or do you not bother with conversation?"

"Shut up," he said, and glanced away.

"Does her dad know?" I watched his face go noticeably paler. "I'm sure Principal Eggrow would just love the idea of his daughter dating the boy who tried to break the record for most detentions."

"Carrie." His voice was low, hard and spoken through unmoving lips. He turned to stare evil beams at me. "It's none of your business. Back off."

Behind us, the front door of the store opened. The bell jingled above it but Marty and I continued to have our stand off. I was sure my expression matched the glaring-eyes, pointed-chin, flaring-nostrils look Marty had.

"You didn't tell her you're the one who dubbed her dear father Mr. Egghead, did you?" I said.

"No. But I told her that last year you taped up pictures of her cousin Rick on the walls of your bedroom."

"Arg! You're such a jerk." I dug my index finger into his chest. He pushed it away with the back his hand. "Go ahead and make a fool of yourself over Abby. I really don't care what you do with her. But why don't you just come home once in a while?"

He rolled his eyes. "Are we back to that again?"

"Well, yeah. That's what I'm doing here in the first place."

Marty sighed and stared at the ceiling for a moment. "Come on, now," he said, and rubbed his eyes as if he were tired. "I'm too old to be living at home. It was time."

I laughed at him with a kind of snort. "I'm not talking about moving back in, bonehead. Heck, I'm glad you're gone and not hogging the bathroom every morning. I'm talking about visits, calls, e-mails, or a message to let Mom and Dad know you're still alive. Sometimes Mom asks me if I heard the phone ring in the other room when the house is perfectly quiet. Now tell me, Marty. Why isn't it ringing? How hard can it be to dial seven little digits? What's so difficult about dropping by for five minutes? It's only four blocks away."

"I have a phone too," he said, "and I never hear it ring."

"Because they think you want to be left alone." I felt like kicking as well as hitting him at this point, just to pound some sense into his void of a head. "Because they think they're respecting your privacy. Quit acting so selfish and stubborn. Make the first move. And quit being such a moron." I slapped a hand over my mouth. My voice had raised a few decibels too high.

I glanced around. Abby and Mrs. Bates had stopped talking and were staring down the aisle at us.

Marty had murder in his eyes as he glared at me. His hands shook as he fisted them at his sides. "Fine," he said. "I'll call her sometime."

I wanted to scream at him. Throw my fists. He looked mad, not sorry or remorseful. Where was the regret? How could he not care? Our parents weren't that terrible. They were strict and old fashioned, yes, but they were fair, and never once had they hidden their love and support for us. They had their faults but what parent didn't? I couldn't understand why he was being so cruel. I used to know him so well, but not anymore.

"Fine," I repeated, and spun away fully intending to stride off with my head held high. But there stood Luke Carter. He was barely inside the store, huddled next to the closed front door, looking awkward and uncomfortable at walking in during the middle of our "family scene."

My heart did a little skip. He was wearing his church clothes: a pale gray, long-sleeved, button-up shirt with a blue tie that had maroon diamonds running in diagonal lines down the front. His shirt was tucked into darker gray, almost charcoal, pleated pants. I could tell he'd shaved since the day before because his jaw was smooth and naked. He looked sleek and expensive and flawless.

I wanted to run and attack him too. I wanted to beat on his chest and demand, "Why'd you hurt me yesterday? Why'd you have to ask me for that stupid walk?"

But then he peered into my eyes, holding his face and his body still. And those eyes of his—those all-too-expressive eyes that crinkled softly—held sadness and compassion. I blinked away a sudden stinging, lowered my head, and began to retreat.

"You forgot your groceries," Marty called.

I paused, keeping my back to him and said, "Why don't you bring them home. That way, *you* can tell Mom yourself, you're not coming for supper."

Then I walked toward the exit. Luke was still there, half blocking my escape. I mumbled an "Excuse me" and he hurried aside—even opened the door for me.

Above us, the bell rang. The sound echoed through my heartbeat. I brushed against Luke's crisp gray sleeve and felt the crinkle of fabric on my elbow. The contact rustled up his smell of clean soap and Right Guard aftershave, a brand that Dad often used. It was familiar, yet disturbingly new and fresh.

I inhaled as much as I could before I was outside and the door closed between us. His smell was washed away, replaced by the chilly autumn and the aroma of dead leaves burning in front yards.

I walked home empty-handed, feeling as lonely as I ever had. I wanted to strangle my brother, but I also wanted to know why I had to feel so defenseless and exposed toward Luke. I wanted to know why he came to visit me at the lot, why he wanted to walk with me in the park, but didn't want to be seen with me. I wasn't that bad of a person. I was by no means popular in school, but I wasn't a total dork.

If I could've paid to get inside his head, I would've stolen money to do so. Instead, I understood nothing. I was angry, confused, lost, excited and scared. I felt all those mixed emotions band my chest, closing snug around my lungs, and I wanted to climb out of my own body so I could escape all the overwhelming sensations.

Too bad I'd left the ice cream behind and couldn't even binge away my misery.

Chapter Four

Turns out Appomattox Court House wasn't a what but a where. Appomattox Court House, Virginia was the name of the town where the Civil War ended. It was where Robert E. Lee, leading the South, met up with Ulysses S. Grant, leading the North. On April 9, 1865, Lee and Grant stood face-to-face in the McLean home and reunited the country, ending the Southern attempt to secede and stopping a war that had already cost more American lives than any other war the United States had fought. What had once been a town, and only the county seat for Appomattox County in Virginia, was now a national park and a legend.

After reading about Appomattox Court House, my mind began to wander. Lying stomach down on my bed, I rested my chin on my hands, stuck my feet in the air, and absorbed the story. I had a layout to put together for the paper and should've forged ahead with that, but I was suddenly very glad Abby had mentioned Appomattox Court House to me. The mysteries behind this town were fascinating. I was curious to find out how such a huge war could end in this small place, which was basically in the middle of nothing. If I'd been alive back in the 1860s, I'm sure my investigative journalism would've taken me right to Appomattox Court House.

This was where it'd all ended, where the dramatic climax of the war came to a head. If Lee hadn't surrendered or if Grant hadn't been civil, things would've turned out differently. The country might not have been united as one any longer.

If I'd been alive, I would've gone to Mr. McLean himself, and quizzed him till his throat was raw. I would've inspected every inch of his farm and the whole town. I mean, it was nothing major, not a capitol or even booming with population. It wasn't an important city at all. It was a "nowhere" just like Stillburrow. And look at what it had become.

It made me think all the nowheres and even the nobodies of the world might stand a chance after all. Suddenly, I felt an uncommon connection with the town in which I lived. It was like I *was* Stillburrow...in a way.

I barely noticed the phone ringing in the other room—maybe because it only got in one ring before Mom snatched it up. I flipped the page of my history book and stared at the picture of the two-story red building where papers had been signed to end the Civil War. I wondered what it would feel like to flip through a history book and see my childhood home on one of these pages were I to ever become famous.

"Carrie?"

I looked up as Mom entered my room with the telephone in her hand. "It's for you," she said. Her eyes held a strange glow.

I wasn't a socialite. I didn't waste time on the telephone and I didn't have any close friends who would bother calling. I knew it couldn't be Marty. He wouldn't want to talk to me. It might be my cousin, Jordan, on the Burke side. She lived with her mother in Paulbrook and we sometimes hung out when she visited her dad every other weekend. But she wasn't around this weekend. I figured it might be my buddy, E.T. But I didn't know what he would want. I only talked to him at school.

Before I could ask though, Mom put her hand over the speaker end of the phone and mouthed two words: *Luke. Carter.*

I could feel my thoughts drain as the blood rushed out of my head. I took the phone. It felt heavy in my hand, weighing like bricks. I stared at the phone as if it were some kind of UFO. This had to be a mistake. But then Mom was pushing it to my ear. She gave me the go-ahead wink. I sent her a *Well, leave me alone* look and she nodded, quickly backing out of the room. When the door quietly clicked shut behind her, I licked my dry lips. My mouth was so close to the receiver, I could almost taste the plastic it was made of.

I sat up and quickly brushed my hair out of my face. I glanced down at my clothing and then stopped, realizing he couldn't see what I looked like.

Finally, I decided I could talk.

"Hello?" I heard my own voice echo along the fiber optic wires. It sounded weird and distant, like I hadn't said it at all but like some kind of echoing radio speaker had spoken for me.

Why in the world was he calling me? I thought I'd never hear from him again after what happened in the park. When Luke spoke, I knew this was really happening, though. It was definitely his voice.

"Did he bring the groceries home?"

I could tell he was smiling by the amused inflection in his voice. He was relaxed, probably on his bed, leaning back against the pillows with his feet stretched out in front of him, legs crossed at the ankles. He wouldn't be wearing his gray church suit anymore but maybe some windbreaker pants and an old cleaned-up practice shirt—white with grass stains on the elbows and a red brave printed across his chest.

"What?" I asked. I shook my head and tried to get the image of Luke Carter sprawled across his bed out of my brain.

"Your brother," he said. "You told him to bring

41

the groceries home. I was just wondering if he ever got around to it."

"Um." I sucked in a breath, hoping it would help bring oxygen back to my brain. "No. He never did."

"Really? And here I was certain he would. I know I definitely would've if you'd laid into me like that."

My mouth fell open. Had Luke Carter just said what I heard him say? Of all the rude things.

"I did not *lay* into him!"

"Oh, yes you did." I could hear him laughing. "I felt sorry for the poor guy. If that's how you usually treat him, I can't blame him for moving out."

Stunned motionless by his words, I instantly retorted, "Marty deserved everything I told him."

"Sure. Just like I deserved your attack yesterday, right?" I could hear him sigh. It sounded like he was stretching out in a hot tub. "You know what I'm beginning to think about you, Carrie Paxton? I think you just like to fight."

I gave a little cry of denial. "You're the one that called and attacked me."

"But it was way too easy to egg you on. So, thank you."

"If you thought that was...Huh? Thank you? Thanks for what?"

"I'll see you in school tomorrow. Bye, Carrie."

"Wait a second."

I thought he'd already hung up, but then he came back. "Hmm? Did you say something?"

"You're dang right I did. What was all that about?"

"You seemed fresh full of fighting today." I pictured him shrugging and flashing his dimple. "Just thought I'd get my jab in."

Luke sounded like he was having fun. I could tell he wasn't mad or bitter. He was purposely baiting me for his own amusement. I frowned.

"What are you doing?" I demanded, and waited for an answer, thumping my foot on the carpet. Luke took his time to respond and I said, "Well?"

Just when I thought I knew what he was about, he went and changed things. My life felt like it was getting crazier and crazier. First I made the mistake of thinking I had a crush on Luke Carter. Then he came to walk in the park with me. And just when I was thinking maybe he liked me back, he hid me to make sure no one saw me with him. And now. Now he was calling me on the phone?

When he spoke, he said it carefully, "I'm not sure what you mean."

"I mean—" I gritted my teeth as I spoke, "what do you mean by calling me?"

"Huh?"

The cry I let out was from pure frustration. Suddenly, I wished Luke Carter was standing right in front of me. So I could choke him. "Just shut up and answer me."

He laughed. It was a husky chuckle and made my stomach tighten. "But how am I supposed to answer if I shut up?"

"Oh my God." I groaned and rubbed at my suddenly aching temples. I had the urge to cry. "Why'd you call me?" I sighed, feeling defeated. "Why'd you come to my Dad's shop yesterday? Why'd you want to walk in the park with me?"

When he was quiet, I went on. "I haven't got a clue what's going on in your mind. But I'm pretty sure you wouldn't want anyone to know we're on the phone right now, just like you didn't want Jill and Liz to see us in the park together. But by calling me, you've really got my mom stirred up. She's probably already got us married off with three kids and a dog named Sparky by now. So why don't you just tell me what you want and leave me alone? Or better yet, just leave me alone."

I thought it was a good speech. I was proud of myself for staying so calm as I delivered it. And I thought it shot straight to the heart of this ever-so-confusing conversation. But what does Mr. Carter say to ruin it all?

He said, "Are you always this honest?"

I thumped my forehead against the palm of my head. "Yes!" I'd never been able to lie in my life, something that absolutely horrified my mother on occasion. But really, what was the use of fibbing? "Now will you please answer me before I scream?"

I could almost see him gnawing on his bottom lip. "Maybe," he replied thoughtfully. "But I can't just yet."

I screamed. I had to lie down on the bed and pull a pillow over my head so my parents wouldn't hear. But I'm sure Luke got an earful. He said a few choice words as I let loose and he probably had to jerk the phone away from his ear and wince.

Afterward, I sat up feeling a little dizzy, but much better. "That's it," I said, and stuck my nose in the air. "I don't have a crush on you anymore, Luke Carter." And for emphasis I sniffed out a little "Humph."

His eyebrows must have shot up on that one because he sounded startled when he said, "You have a crush on me?"

"No," I replied regally. "I just said I didn't."

"But you did before?" I had him completely baffled. "I thought I heard your brother say you had Rick Getty's picture all over your wall."

I cringed. Just how much had he heard in the store? Oh well, I'd worry about that later. "That was last year," I said. "You're the hot topic this year."

"*Me?*" I didn't think he was trying to be vain and draw compliments out of me, because the poor boy honestly sounded confused.

I loved it.

"But why?"

"Please." I gave the word two syllables as I snorted it. "You're good looking, rich, unattached, popular, and fairly intelligent. Why wouldn't every girl dream about you?"

"But why do you? You don't seem like the type to follow the pack."

I shrugged. I'd already spilled this first part. Why not let him know everything? It wasn't like I still had a crush on him anymore, right?

"Since that football interview," I said, "I kept running into you and having the oddest meetings. So you got stuck in my head, and I was forced to think about you. From there, it just seemed to grow. And let's not forget the whole park incident."

"All I did was hold your hand and push you on the swing. Geez, Carrie. It's not that big of a deal."

"But it doesn't take Luke Carter much to charm a nobody like me."

"Don't say that about yourself. You're not a nobody." For the first time since I'd picked up the phone, I heard irritation in his voice.

"Watch what you say," I warned. "Any more compliments and you'll have my geeky heart going pitter-pat all over again."

"Cut it out."

I laughed, giving it a wicked sound. "What's wrong, Lucas? Every other girl in school thinks you're the hottest thing since the microwave."

"They do not!" He was spitting out denials desperately. "And don't call me that."

"Are you blushing?" I said, knowing I had full control of the conversation.

"No."

"You are." I giggled. "Oh, this is precious. I'm making Luke Carter blush."

"Stop it, Carrie." His voice carried heat and a warning. "This is weird."

"I take it that the reason you keep bugging me has nothing to do with romantic intentions, then?"

There was a pause. And then, "Of course not," he said with such emphasis, it suddenly had my brain whirling.

No romantic intentions, huh? It hurt. I can't deny it. But I was too curious to let a thing like that bother me. Remember, I'm an investigative journalist at heart. I was going to get to the bottom of this. If the guy was going to break my heart I was going to find out why.

"Hmm," I said, and tapped my chin.

"What?"

I smiled when I heard alarm in his voice. "I'm thinking."

"OK, now you're scaring me." He didn't sound scared, but wary. Very, very wary. "What're you thinking?"

"I'm thinking of what I might possibly have that you want?"

"I don't—"

"No, no." I grinned, knowing I had him nervous. "Let me guess here." By the way he sounded, I knew I had to be getting close to his secret intentions.

"You don't want me for my body," I said, ignoring a pang of self-pity over that fact. "You showed interest in one of my Dad's cars. But it's obvious you don't really want to buy one of them. I suppose you could be somehow trying to infiltrate my father's business and take it over. But that can't be it, since your dad already owns more of it than my dad does."

"Carrie, don't—" I could tell it made him uncomfortable to mention Dad's debt to his father at the bank. I hurried on, interrupting him.

"So that can't be it," I said. "But then I see you at the grocery store today and that makes me think of Abby Eggrow."

"Abby Eggrow?" He laughed. "OK, I've got to hear this one."

"All right." I cracked my knuckles. "Marty's been seen publicly with Abby lately. But wait! Luke suddenly thinks he's interested in her. He's jealous of Marty Paxton and needs to come up with some way to get Marty out of the picture. So first he goes to visit Marty's home. He talks to the dad and then to the sister to see if he can pressure some information out of them and discover some kind of weakness in Marty. But he comes up with a blank. So he strolls into Getty's General this afternoon to put the moves on Abby himself."

I thought it was a viable solution. Granted, I'd just thought it up and I hadn't worked out any of the kinks yet. But it might be why Luke kept bugging me.

"So what do you think?" I asked.

Luke said, "I think you read too many Nancy Drew mysteries."

I frowned. "It's not Abby then, huh?"

"Definitely not." Luke seemed more adamant about his secret not being romantic intentions toward Abby than he'd been adamant about it not being romantic intentions toward me. It was a small victory for me, but it made me feel smug nonetheless.

"OK," I said. "Then how about this?"

"I'm not sure if I want to hear anymore." But I could tell he did. It was amusing him. And I was having fun myself.

I squeezed my eyes tight and thought desperately. What would Luke Carter want from me? I wasn't beautiful. I wasn't smart and I didn't have any special talents...Wait a second. What was my one talent?

I was so excited I jumped to my feet. "It's because I write."

Luke said nothing so I knew instantly I'd struck oil. I slapped a hand to my head. "That's it. It all makes sense now. In the park, you kept asking me about my writing."

"So?" He couldn't hide the little twitter of desperation he felt. I could hear it in the quiver of his vocal cords as he struggled to sound insolent. I don't know why he was trying to hide it. Maybe there was something else he still didn't want me to know.

"So," I echoed. "Why would you care about my writing, unless..." I snapped my fingers. "Unless it could be used as some kind of service to you."

"Look, Carrie. This is getting crazy. I'm going to hang up."

I had to be really close now.

"You want me to write a paper for you." Yes, I had it all figured out. He was embarrassed to come right out and ask me. He didn't know if I was the type to outright refuse him and then go tell the teacher he wanted to cheat. He must've been testing me to see what sort of person I was. And he still wasn't sure if he could put his trust in me yet.

It made me feel good to think he wanted to use my writing ability. Writing was one of the most important parts of my life. I liked the idea of having a talent desired by others.

"You want me to write a paper for you," I repeated with more confidence. "Don't you?"

"No." He said it with such force I almost believed him. And then there was a click.

My mouth fell open. "What the..." I stared at the dead phone for a second. Then I knotted my jaw and hit *69. He answered two rings later.

I knew he had caller ID because he spat out, "What?"

I grinned and said, "Liar."

Then I hung up on him.

Chapter Five

"Miss Paxton. Can I have a word with you?"

I closed my eyes and slid further into my seat. The bell had just rung, dismissing class. I should've been free to go, free from dreaded trigonometry. My teacher, however, thought otherwise. I was tempted to tell Mr. Underhill—or Mr. Under-the-Hill as Marty'd always called him—that no, he could not have a word with me. But I knew that wouldn't go over so swell. So I gave a miserable nod and gathered my books.

I'd just taken my history test the hour before. And Mr. Decker hadn't asked a single question about Appomattox Court House. I glared at Abby Eggrow for misguiding me when I passed her in the hall. But she was busy gossiping with Jill and Liz and didn't notice me at all. Big surprise, huh?

And then I'd gotten to trig only to realize we had an assignment due—an assignment I'd completely forgotten about. Of course.

I'd arrived early, sat in the back next to E.T., and waited for Luke to arrive. I had no idea what to expect from him. OK, I did have one idea. I expected him to completely ignore me. And I wasn't wrong.

He was chatting with Nathan Bates when he strolled in. His book bag was slung over his shoulder and he smiled, showing off that stunning dimple. I stared at him so hard I bore a hole through him. And I know he saw me too because he searched the room when he entered. He even made eye contact with me

49

as he scanned but he didn't stop, just kept scanning until he caught sight of some football players across the room. He and Nathan went to sit with them. E.T. was rambling off something in my ear. He sounded eager about what he was saying.

"So...what do you think?" he finally paused to ask.

I glanced at him. "I think you sound like an adult on a *Peanuts* show. All I heard was blah, blah, blah."

Thank goodness E.T. was used to my being so blunt. He was a good buddy—the biggest geek I'd ever met—but a good buddy. E.T. Fitz, short for Elmer Theodore Fitz, was the prime target for ridicule at SEC. First of all, he was unlucky enough to be the middle son of Mr. and Mrs. Fitz who ran the funeral home in Stillburrow, which meant he grew up in a house where corpses were laid out in his basement on a regular basis. Plus, he was named Elmer. And since his last name started with an F, circumstances begged he be called Elmer Fudd. But the jokes didn't stop there.

Elmer was a genius. He was the president of the math club and if SEC had boasted a history or chess club, he would've been president of them too. He was proud of his wits, though. He once told me when I was sitting by him in the lunchroom, that at times he felt so smart he thought his head would explode from all the knowledge it contained. I told him to grow up. Then I took his chocolate milk and drank it.

Elmer endured the ridicule very well. Usually, he didn't understand he was the brunt of the laughter. Either that or he ignored it with style. After seeing the movie *E.T.: The Extra-Terrestrial* for the first time, he decided he wanted to be referred to as E.T. from then on. He declared it was his favorite movie and it had remained his favorite ever since. He was so excited he already had the initials for it, he went around telling everyone to call him that.

His classmates heartily agreed, because he kind of looked like the alien with his short legs and overly big head. E.T. never caught on that he was actually being made fun of whenever someone used his nickname, and I didn't have the heart to tell him. So the name stuck. And he liked it. Therefore, I couldn't complain.

Despite his braininess, E.T. sometimes seemed like the senile family pet—partly deaf and limping around on three legs. Everyone complained about him but no one had the heart to put him out of his misery. I had to love him, though. He was my best friend.

"About journalism class," E.T. was saying, snapping me back to attention. "I think we should move the survey I took about who believes in ghosts to page one."

I made a face of horror. It took me hours to figure out where to place each article in *The Central Record*. And I became a tad testy when anyone questioned the end results of my layouts.

"I've already set Miss Bowman's retirement announcement to page one," I told him with a voice that demanded he not disagree.

He put on his thinking face, where he scrunched up his mouth and wrinkled his nose. I prepared to shoot down any idea he had, so when all he said was a thoughtful, "Oh," I had to pause a second before I realized he wasn't going to argue with me.

But as soon as I let out a sigh of relief, he said, "Can we switch it with the sports section, then?"

I snorted. "Yeah, right. That'd go over real well."

"But we're between seasons. Football and volleyball are over for the year and basketball hasn't even had a game yet."

"I don't care," I said. "We're not moving sports to

51

the back page."

Actually, I agreed with E.T. on this score. The only things we had for the sports section in our next issue were a few pictures of the first day of basketball practice and a couple of quotes from the coach about how he thought the year would turn out. But I wasn't stupid. Sports were a big—no, a *huge*—deal to the citizens of Stillburrow. Putting the sports section on the very back page, where obituaries were usually kept, would be like digging my own grave. Every parent and child who went to any sports game (and that was about ninety percent of the town) would throw a fit if the sports section was moved from its usual spot on page two. I'd probably lose my editing post.

But I never got around to explaining this to E.T. because Under-the-hill started class and asked everyone to pass their assignments forward. Quickly I whispered to E.T., asking which assignment that was. But Under-the-hill caught me talking and said, "Miss Paxton, where's your assignment?"

So then the entire class grew quiet and stared at me, which made me search for the nearest place to hide. I could tell I even had Luke's attention because I knew what his stare felt like.

Mumbling, I admitted I'd forgotten about the assignment and Under-the-hill went into a ten-minute lecture on forgetfulness. All the while, I sunk deeper and deeper into my chair.

That should've been the end of my horror. I certainly thought it served as an overly just punishment. But no. Under-the-hill had to call me up to his desk to stay after class as well.

People glanced at me as they shuffled out. I waited till my row was clear before I approached his desk, but not everyone was gone. Luke was still across the room, gathering his supplies. I swore he was dawdling on purpose to hear me get ripped into.

But I just wanted the speech to get underway and over with, so I ignored Carter's presence.

Under-the-hill sighed wearily when he looked up at me. He slid off his glasses and rubbed his nose. "Miss Paxton, need I remind you what your grade is in this class?"

I shuffled the pile of books in my arms because they suddenly felt heavy. "No."

"This class is primarily for seniors. I've let a few juniors join only because I thought they were ready. Now I had my doubts about you but you're usually a hard worker..."

I gritted my teeth and silently cursed E.T. for pressuring me into taking this stupid course with him. He'd been all gung-ho for trigonometry and he'd begged me to take it too.

I saw Luke across the room, finally rising from his chair and I glared, but he managed to keep his gaze from mine. The coward.

"...I seriously recommend you seek a tutor."

My head swiveled back to Under-the-hill. "What?"

A tutor? The man was calling me stupid? In front of Luke? I felt my face heat.

"No, that's OK," I said. "I can do better. I don't need a tutor. Really."

Under-the-hill eyed me critically. "I don't think you understand what I'm saying, Miss Paxton." He stared me down. I stared back. And then he dropped the bomb. "Get a tutor, or I drop you from the class."

My lips fell apart as I gaped at him. He couldn't do that. Dropped from a class? What would I do? I needed a math credit, and I'd be too far behind to enter another class. I'd have to take two math courses next year.

No way.

"But, Mr. Under-the...I mean, Underhill—"

At my slip, his eyes narrowed and his lips

pursed. "My decision is final, Miss Paxton."

My mouth worked but no words came out. I wanted to scream. Why would he do this to me? It was beyond torture. I didn't go to other people for help. I always did my own work.

Then I thought of E.T. and calmed immediately. E.T. didn't know how to tutor. He always sped ahead and never could slow down to explain why he was doing what he did. That was why I never studied with him. But I could spend an hour with him and tell Under-the-hill I was being tutored. Then I'd just work harder and improve my grades on my own. I was about to nod and say, "OK, I'll find someone to help me," when an all-too-familiar voice behind me broke in.

"I'll give her a hand."

I whipped around so fast it made Luke jump back a step. The rest of the class had cleared out. Only the three of us—Under-the-hill, Luke, and I—remained in the room.

"Ah, Mr. Carter." Under-the-hill sat forward, slipped his glasses back on and flipped through his grade book. After checking Luke's scores, he nodded. "Yes. I think that would work out quite well. Miss Paxton?" He glanced at me.

I had the refusal on the tip of my tongue but the awful teacher didn't even give me a chance to refuse. He simply said, "Settle on a time to meet with Mr. Carter, would you?"

I stared at him. Then I looked up at Luke. This was a joke, right?

"I could come to your house right after school today," Luke offered.

My eyes bugged. Right after school? Today?
No!

"That sounds great," Under-the-hill answered for me as he rose. He patted me on the back as if sending me on my way.

I glared at Luke. He smiled, flaunting his arrogant dimple, then turned and strolled out of the room, whistling.

I was left there, sputtering and going into the shock of a lifetime. But neither Luke nor Under-the-hill seemed to notice or care. I was stuck. Luke Carter was going to be my trigonometry tutor. And I didn't have any say-so about it.

Chapter Six

"You're mad, aren't you?"

I slammed the door behind me and glared up at Luke as I flung my book bag to the floor next to his. "Let's just get this over with."

He stood in the middle of my living room, and as thrilling as it felt to see him there, I was still furious with him. I had no idea what had possessed him into volunteering to be my tutor. Maybe he thought he could use it as some kind of leverage to get me to write a paper for him. I didn't know for sure. All I knew was that at that moment I wasn't willing to write a single word for him.

Still, he looked good. His dark hair stood out noticeably against the light tones in my mother's ivory living room. I watched him turn and stare at my home. What he saw was a pristine room. The couch was a bit faded, but every cushion, pillow, and ruffle sat in its proper place. There were no papers or magazines in sight—only a dusted coffee table with a single candle in the center. On a bookcase by the television, novels and videocassettes lined the shelves in order from largest to smallest. There were no smudges on any glass surface and there were dark and light lines on the carpet from a recent vacuuming.

Mom had wanted to redecorate the year before, but Dad said it was a waste of good money. Mom ran to my Great Aunt Kay to complain. So Aunt Kay decided to buy herself new furniture, and she said she would let us have her old cream-colored set. It was a step up for us, but Mom still wasn't satisfied. Dad budged a little though and let her paint the walls.

"Whoa," Luke said. He ran his hand over a corner table and then examined his fingers. They came away clean and free of dust.

"I know." I stood next to him, temporarily forgetting my irritation. "I told my mom she would make millions if she ever started her own cleaning service."

"She would," he agreed. "I know my mom would hire her instantly. She's not very happy with the cleaning lady we have now."

Leave it to him to mention his family could afford a cleaning service.

"Thanks a lot."

Luke turned to stare at me. He seemed surprised to hear my tone of voice. "What?"

I looked away and started for the kitchen. "Nothing."

He followed me. I could feel him right behind me. "No. That was definitely something. What'd I say?"

I spun around so quickly he had to pull up short to keep from plowing into me. The distance between us was close enough I had to move back a step to stay mad. Otherwise, I would've melted right there at his feet.

"I already realize your family is so much better off than mine. And I already know you could afford a cleaning lady while my family probably should be cleaning houses to put more money toward our debts. I'm also well aware of the fact I'm poor and you're rich, OK. So you don't have to rub it in."

"*What?!*" Luke grabbed my arm. "I didn't mean that."

I pulled away to ground my fisted hands onto

my hips and glare up at him. "But didn't you?"

"Absolutely not," he insisted. I watched him squint his eyes and grit his teeth. "I wasn't thinking of money at all when I said it. And I wasn't trying to rub anything in."

He pointed a finger at my nose and stepped closer, towering over me until I had to crane my head back to see the fury in his eyes. "I'm sick of you always attacking me. Who cares about who has more money? It doesn't make a bit of difference about anything."

"Oh yeah," I said. "I bet you know exactly how much my daddy owes your daddy."

Luke took a step away, breathing heavily. He ran his hand through his hair, letting the black locks fall wildly. When he eyed me again, he seemed a bit calmer. "He doesn't owe my dad anything. If he has a debt, then it's with the bank."

"But you know what his debt is, don't you?" When Luke's face flushed, I shot back. "You do!"

"Oh, who cares what I know," Luke said, his voice growing louder. "It doesn't mean anything."

"It does," I said. "It's important."

Luke stopped his argument then. He stared at me for a second, taking in my red face, my rising and falling chest, and my fisted hands. His shoulders dropped and he said, "You know, Carrie, it's only important because you're making it important."

I looked away, a little guilty, and I crossed my arms self-consciously. "I'm not the only one. Everybody in this whole town puts value on who owns what and who makes what."

"And since when do you care what everybody else thinks?"

I looked at him, bewildered. I wanted to say, "Since I learned I was a nobody and not good enough for you," but he started in again.

"From way back in grade school, I remember you

as the one who rolled your eyes at what everyone else did and then went off to do your own thing. When Jill Anderson called E.T. Fitz 'Elmer Fudd' you were the one that gave her a black eye and became his personal defender. You were the one who showed up in a bright green dress on 'All Red' spirit day."

I grinned. "That was good, wasn't it?"

Luke smiled too. "I'll never forget the look on Principal Eggrow's face when he saw you strolling down the hall dressed like an undecorated Christmas tree."

I beamed up at him. We were standing so close, I had this powerful urge to wrap my arms around his neck and hug him for making me feel better. And I was about to do just that. I could feel myself drawing closer when I realized what I was doing. I jumped back, coughed into my hand and started for the refrigerator

"OK, you're right." I looked up and caught the gleam of triumph in his eyes. "This time, anyway," I added before dropping my gaze. "And I'm sorry I overreacted about the money issue."

"Are you going to stop making me feel like I owe you something because of it?" I nodded and he said, "Because I can't help who my parents are, anymore than you can control who yours are."

"I know," I said, and bent my head even more. "I'm sorry." Sheesh, he had this terrific ability to make me feel like a jerk.

"All right, then. I'm glad we got that straight."

But I couldn't raise my head. Everything I'd said to him was suddenly replaying in my head.

"Hey," he said softly, and bumped my arm with his shoulder. I looked up. "Don't worry about it anymore, all right?"

I nodded but I couldn't speak. I still couldn't believe how rude I'd been. Sure, I was honest but that didn't mean I had to intentionally say something to hurt another person. Well, unless it was Marty. And this guy was by no means my brother.

"What've you got to eat in here, anyway?" he said. I'd moved to the fridge but hadn't gotten around to opening it. So he seized the initiative for me. It took me a second to realize he was trying to smooth us out of an awkward moment. But when I did, I fell for him even harder. And I completely forgot about why I'd been so angry with him in the first place.

Luke rested his arm on the top of the opened refrigerator door and leaned down to peer inside. I caught myself staring at him, noticing how nice he looked when he leaned over. I turned away, blushing, glad he couldn't read my thoughts.

And that's when I saw the note lying on the counter next to a bowl of fruit. It was from my mother, telling me she'd gone to Paulbrook to buy a birthday present for Aunt Kay.

That meant I was alone in the house with Luke.

Suddenly jittery in the stomach, I reached for the fruit bowl on the counter, knowing I needed to keep my nervous fingers busy or they'd shake right off my hands. I pulled out a banana, peeled it, and took a bite just as Luke stood up empty-handed. When he saw my food of choice, he gave me an odd look.

"No wonder you're so skinny."

I shrugged and looked at my banana. "What?"

"Carrie, Carrie, Carrie," he said on a disapproving sigh. "This is the prime time of the day for a person to splurge on junk food." He spoke seriously, as if it was a sacred belief, and I had to giggle. But he didn't catch the humor.

"Think about it," he said. "Adults stuff that nutritious garbage down us three times a day. Right after the bell rings and we've gained our freedom, we need a little brain food to recoup." He stopped lecturing then and just shook his head like I was hopeless. I took another bite and he grabbed the banana from me.

"Hey. I'm not done with that."

"Yes, you are." He found a trashcan and threw my snack away.

When he returned, I set my hands on my hips. "What do you think you're doing?"

"Here." He grabbed my shoulders and ushered me to a chair, pushing me into it. "Sit. I see you need a lesson. So I'm going to demonstrate how to make a *true* after-school snack."

I was stunned. Before my very eyes, Luke Carter turned into some kind of Betty Crocker, opening cabinets and pulling down boxes and jars.

"Make yourself at home," I said dryly. But then I became too fascinated with watching him to comment further.

I had no idea what he was making but the ingredients were vanilla wafers, creamy peanut butter, and chocolate syrup. When he pulled open the freezer door and hauled out a tub of vanilla ice cream, I wrinkled my nose. What was he doing? Luke found a bowl in one of the cabinets and started to create his masterpiece. First, he piled on three huge scoops of ice cream and then he spread the peanut butter over it like frosting. He lined the top with vanilla wafers and then he artistically applied the syrup. When he was done he stepped back, grinning.

"Now *this* is an after-school snack."

I gaped at the formation he'd built. "You're not actually going to eat that, are you?"

He flashed his dimples. "Nope. You are. I'm going to make my own."

I surged to my feet. "No way." I couldn't eat that

much in a whole day.

Luke's back faced me as he searched a row of drawers. Either he didn't hear what I said or he simply ignored me because he said, "Where's your silverware drawer?"

He pulled open one drawer and found it full of wine bottles. He slipped one out and cradled it in his hands while he read the label. Then he glanced over toward me and wiggled his eyebrows. When I shook my head, he called me a party pooper and put it back, only to pull open the next drawer.

"Don't you people use silverware around here?"

"Not at all," I answered, rolling my eyes and sweeping open a drawer near me. "We eat with our bare hands like the uncouth *savages* we Paxtons are."

Luke spun around to glare at me but when he saw I'd opened the drawer he was looking for, he marched over and yanked out a spoon. He held it two inches in front of my face and nodded toward the bowl. "Eat."

I stuck my tongue out at him. It was immature but it had his face going purple and his jaw clenching.

Then his shoulders dropped. He sighed. "Come on, Carrie. I made it just for you. You could at least try it."

I glanced at the melting mass of ice cream and other assorted goods. Food heaped in a mound three inches higher than the rim. I winced. "Make me a smaller version and I might."

His face instantly brightened. "One smaller version coming up."

He hummed while he whipped up another bowl, one that was significantly smaller but still looked like too much. When he set it in front of me, I made a face.

He growled. "You said you'd try it."

I glared up at him. "I said I might," I reminded him. But then I saw the hint of a wounded expression and melted. "I want to see you take a bite of yours first."

His injured look flashed back into a smile. "Oh ye of little faith," he said, and to prove his snack worthy, he picked up his bowl. I watched him shovel in a large bite and almost gagged. But the abundant volume he consumed didn't seem to bother Luke. He moaned and made sounds of pleasure. "Told you it was good."

I snickered. "You know you look totally stupid doing that, don't you?" I lied. He really looked adorable, but I wasn't about to let him know that.

He stopped with the sounds and gave me a dirty look. When I didn't even attempt to try my share, he dished out a spoonful for me. My stomach did a little flip-flop when he held it up to my mouth, but there was no way I could refuse that bite. I opened up and squeezed my eyes shut. He muttered the word *coward* as he gave me a taste. I took my first mouthful. Cold ice cream and warm peanut butter mixed with the crunchy wafers. It was a different sensation than I expected but it grew on me. My teeth clinked on stainless steel as Luke pulled the spoon free. I heard him scoop up a second bite. OK, so it wasn't bad.

I opened my eyes and caught Luke watching me intently. When I shrugged, he chuckled. "I bet you wouldn't admit it if this was the best thing you ever tasted."

I swallowed and dabbed at the corner of my mouth for crumbs. "It was fine," I said in my prim-and-proper voice.

"You loved it," he retorted.

"I said it was good. What more do you want?"

Luke continued to stare at me as if he expected an attack. I lifted my chin, meeting his challenging gaze. He really did have pretty eyes. The blue in them was so pure. But as I stared at them longer, I began to find little golden specks in the blue. And the black iris part had these lighter lines that angled in toward the center. I'd never examined someone's eyes so closely. Then I noticed he was staring at me just as intently.

I turned away slightly, dropping my gaze, and heard Luke clear his throat.

From the corner of my eyes, I saw him rub the back of his neck. "I thought we were supposed to be studying trigonometry," he said.

I nodded, still unable to meet his gaze. "I'll go get our bags."

I pressed my hand over my heart as I raced back into the living room. "Calm down, Carrie. Just...breathe." But I felt exhilarated. I wanted to dance. Luke Carter was in my house. He made me food, he spoon-fed me, and stood close enough to kiss me. There was no way I could calm down. I fanned my hot face, but it was useless. I was definitely smitten with the guy. Smitten? An old fashioned word, yes, but it suited the situation perfectly.

"Where's your room?" I heard him call from the kitchen.

I grabbed our packs and stood quickly, my eyes growing wide. "Why?" I yelled back, hoping desperately he wasn't searching for it, that he hadn't already found the pigsty which I called my lair.

"Isn't that where we're going to study?"

I raced to the kitchen and slumped against the doorframe when I saw him still there, leaning against the counter and gobbling down his ice cream creation. "What's wrong with the kitchen table," I said, winded from my run.

He glanced up, set his bowl down on the table, and strolled over to slide his book bag off my shoulder. "What's wrong with your room?" he countered.

"I'm not going to let you see my room. Are you crazy?"

His eyebrows shot up and he took a startled step back. "I guess so."

I plopped my heavy bag on the kitchen table with a thud and took a seat. Luke shrugged and sat next to me. I tried to ignore how close he was, but when his knee brushed mine under the table, my stomach took notice and started to churn.

"So how far are you behind?"

I winced while I pulled out my trig notebook and flipped it open. "I'm not sure. I started to get lost after the first week of class."

Luke blew out a breath. "Great," he said with a healthy lack of enthusiasm. He sighed and reached for my notebook. "OK, let's check out the damage."

As he scanned my homework pages, I grabbed my ice cream and jammed a spoonful into my mouth nervously. It was one thing to have your crush in your home. It was another to let him see how awful you were doing in a class. And I could tell I was doing pretty badly by the way he kept wincing.

"First of all," he said, "you should really do this in pencil. It's easier and a lot cleaner to erase, instead of having all these mark-out lines confusing you."

"OK," I said.

He looked at me expectantly. "OK," he repeated. "Where's your pencil?"

"Oh...right." I jumped from my chair. "Ah, let me go get one."

When I finally found one, I could tell he was laughing at me.

"What?"

"I can't believe you're a writer and you don't have a pencil," he said.

I shrugged. "I use pens."

Linda Kage

After that, we got down to business. Luke polished off his sundae thing and when I was full he finished mine too. I was surprised to discover how good a tutor he was. He went through each step with me and if I didn't understand something, he explained it until I did. I was actually beginning to comprehend trigonometry by the time the back door opened.

Luke and I lifted our heads at the same time to watch Dad step inside. He was wearing his shop coveralls and looking dog-tired. I popped to my feet and grabbed the two empty bowls off the table as if they were some kind of incriminating evidence. I'd completely lost track of time and I think Luke had too because I saw him rub his eyes and check the clock on the wall.

"Hi, Dad," I said.

"Hello." His voice was chalky and garbled, like that was the first time he'd used it all day. And if he hadn't spoken today, then he probably hadn't had any customers to speak to. Ergo, business had been slow. He scrubbed his feet on the welcome mat, knowing Mom would scalp him if he left dirt on the floor, all the while his gaze darted between Luke and me.

Unable to meet his eyes for some reason, I lowered my face and noticed what I was still holding. I rushed the bowls to the sink and began rinsing them. When I decided they were clean and it was safe enough to face my father without my cheeks going tomato red, I turned slowly and managed a half grin.

"Missed you in the shop today," he said, and his gaze slid to the source of the reason. Luke shifted and shoved his hands into his pockets.

I stepped forward. "Luke was helping me with my trigonometry." It sounded like I was trying to cover something up, which I wasn't because that was

66

the God's honest truth. Luke *had* been helping me with my trigonometry.

My dad just nodded and stared.

Luke closed his notebook and shoved it into his bag. "Hi, Mr. Paxton," he said in a friendly fashion, but the speed with which he packed his things made us look just as guilty. And there was nothing for us to be guilty about.

So I said, "Mr. Underhill said I had to have a tutor. So..." I glanced at Luke.

Dad nodded again and rocked back on his heels, remaining on the safety of the floor mat. Luke glanced from him to me and, for a moment, we all three just kind of stood there. Only my dad, I thought, would know how to show up at the worst possible time and ruin a great moment I was having.

Luke hiked his bag onto his shoulder and said to me, "I better get going."

I nodded. "OK."

He started for the living room and I followed. Finally, my father began to thaw. He waved at Luke and smiled, saying, "Thanks for giving Carrie a hand with her homework."

I wanted to growl at him for being too late with his friendliness, but Luke returned the smile and said, "No problem."

In the living room, it was just the two of us. He turned back before leaving. "Same time tomorrow?"

I nodded. I knew if I said yes it would sound way too enthusiastic. So I just swallowed my excitement and smiled at him demurely even though I'm sure my eyes were sparkling and my lips were drawn thin from the grin I was repressing.

He nodded too and turned away. At that moment, he looked like the great football player he was. Even though the season was over, he still had those stiff, jerky movements like he was carrying heavy pads on his shoulders. The book bag bunched the muscles across his back, and since his shirt was stretched tight from the weight straining against it, I could see every detail. I was transfixed. He reached for the door handle and I wanted to grab his hand, come up with some excuse to waylay him a few seconds longer. But my mind was blank.

Suddenly, the knob turned in his hand and the door flew inward. In swept my mother, her arms full of sacks. Luke, with his quick reflexes, jumped back. When Mom saw him, she skidded to a halt, barely avoiding a collision.

"Oh," she said, breathless. "I'm sorry. Did I hit you?"

Luke shook his head. "No. You're fine. I was just leaving."

"Oh," Mom repeated and slid out of his way. "Goodbye, then."

"Bye." He glanced at me one more time before closing the door.

When it shut, the room seemed to suck in around me. I noticed Dad had come to the living room doorway and was leaning against it. Mom, with her arms filled, blinked at me.

"He was tutoring me for trigonometry class," I said.

Mom smiled politely but her eyes said she knew better. "Well, that was nice of him."

I didn't like her tone of voice at all. So I lied. "Mr. Underhill *asked* him to," I added. "He said I needed a tutor and he asked Luke."

I could tell she didn't believe me. "Why didn't he ask your friend, Elmer?"

"Because Elmer sucks at tutoring," I shot back, a bit too loudly. "He couldn't teach a bee to buzz. And since Luke gets good grades too, Mr. Underhill asked him." Mom and Dad continued to watch me with that funny *Whatever you say, Honey* expression.

I had to come to my own defense. "We were

doing homework," I said heavily. "That's all."

"I wasn't asking," she answered, unable to hide the mischievous gleam in her eye.

"I'm not kidding," I insisted. "That's all there is to it. Nothing else is going on. So don't think there is, OK?"

"Fine," she said. But when she looked at Dad, they shared a grin that seemed to say, *Our baby girl's growing up.*

I muttered that my parents were ridiculous. They laughed. Balling my hands into fists, I stomped off to the sanity of my room.

Chapter Seven

"You know what I don't understand?" E.T. said.

"What's that?" I asked before taking a bite of my salad. It was hot dog day in the lunchroom and I couldn't stand hot dogs. I'd opted to buy a salad, but they'd run out of my favorite dressing by the time I'd made it to the front of the line. Go figure. So there I was, stuck eating a plain-Jane salad with my dorky friend.

Across from me, E.T. took a bite of his hot dog. Ketchup squirted out the end and sprayed in my direction.

"Hey," I yelped. "Watch where you're aiming that thing." I found a napkin and wiped the red blob on the tabletop between us.

"Sorry." E.T. flipped his dog around to mop up the drip from the end of his bun, but sent another glob of ketchup flying. This time it landed on his white button-up shirt.

I groaned and cradled my forehead in my hand, shaking my face from side to side. "It's hopeless," I murmured to myself. When I looked up, he'd managed to get some on his thick glasses as well. "Just stop now," I said, holding up my hands for him to halt. He'd started to dab at his shirt but only succeeded in smearing it pathetically. "E.T., stop!"

He paused and lifted his head.

I held out my hand, palm up. "Give me your glasses."

"Why?"

"Because you have ketchup all over them. And quit wiping your shirt. You're making it worse." E.T. glanced down like he was tempted to ignore me. "Trust me," I said. "A napkin's not going to get that stain out."

He sighed. His shoulders sank in defeat and he let his wadded napkin fall on the table. He ripped off his glasses and tossed them at me. "Why does this always happen to me?"

"Quit complaining." I wiped one lens clean and started on the other. "It could be worse."

E.T. used both hands to point at the front of his shirt. "How could this be any worse?"

I glanced up and grinned. "It could've happened to me."

"Funny," he said dryly.

"I thought so." I handed the clean lenses back and watched him slip them on. "You were saying?"

"I was?" He glanced at his hot dog as if it possessed all the answers. "Oh yeah. I don't understand why Mr. Underhill asked Luke Carter to tutor you and he didn't ask me."

My fork slipped out of my hand and clattered to the tabletop. "Say what?"

But E.T. didn't answer. Brenda Newell just had to walk into the cafeteria at that exact moment. She was strolling hand-in-hand with Rick Getty. But that didn't stop E.T. from pausing everything he was doing to gawk at her.

The year before, he and I had been quite the pair. He'd had a crush on Brenda, and I had one on Rick. E.T. had fallen for Brenda in the first grade when she sang "Silent Night" in the Christmas program. Since then, he went to every music concert the school put on and stopped whatever he was doing just to watch her walk by. I hadn't been that crazy about Rick. I just thought he was cute. He used to sit next to me in English class and make fun of the teacher. He cracked the most hilarious jokes. But then he and Brenda started dating and he quit paying attention to me. That was when I ripped all the pictures of him off my wall. I had to admit, though, he and Brenda looked cute together. They were a good fit.

Today however, I was preoccupied with what E.T.'d just said. I made a disgusted sound and snapped my fingers twice in front of his face. "Hello? Earth to Elmer."

"Hmm?" He transferred his look to me. His eyes were still glazed over and his goofy smile appeared to be stuck. But then he caught my look and straightened. "What'd you say?"

"I wasn't saying anything. You were."

"Oh...right. I...?" His eyes scanned the room again in search of his fair lady.

I rolled my eyes. "How'd you know Luke was tutoring me?" I said, breaking into his daze.

E.T. gave up on his Brenda search and sighed as he picked up a tater tot. "I heard him talking in the bathroom." He took a bite and must've decided it needed ketchup too, because he picked up a package with a tomato printed on it and started to rip it open.

In the hope of avoiding another ketchup disaster, I snatched the package from him and opened it. Handing it back, I said, "And?"

"And what?"

I made a screeching sound through my gritted teeth. "And what did he say about it?"

"Nothing." E.T. shrugged. "His friend...What's his name? The sheriff's son."

"Nathan Bates."

E.T. snapped his fingers. "Yeah, Nathan. Nate asked Luke where he was last night and Luke told him about Mr. Underhill making him tutor you."

I gaped at my ketchup-stained friend. "He *said*

that?"

E.T. nodded. "Why'd Mr. Underhill ask him and not me?" E.T. looked hurt. But that wasn't my main concern. I reached across the table and grabbed him by the collar.

"Is that exactly what he said? That Under-the-hill *asked* him to tutor me?"

Again E.T. just nodded. He seemed unconcerned that I was dragging him half across the table. "You don't think he's making a higher grade than me, do you?"

I let go of E.T., and he dropped back onto his bench. "Of course not," I said, suddenly feeling sorry for him. E.T. would be crushed if a super jock was pulling a better average than he was. All E.T. had to fall back on were his brains. And if that failed, he probably thought he had nothing. I quickly concocted an explanation to soothe him.

"I bet he asked Carter because he's a senior and you're just a junior," I said. E.T.'s shoulders eased so I guessed that did the trick.

"Yeah," he said. "That's probably it. Besides, if Luke's tutoring you for extra bonus points then he can't be making *that* awesome a grade."

I surged to my feet, causing E.T. to jump. He gaped up at me.

"He said that too?" I demanded.

E.T. shrank back, knowing the enraged look in my eyes only too well. He nodded meekly as if I might whip him for giving the wrong answer.

"He said...he said Mr. Underhill offered to give him bonus points to tutor you."

"Bonus points?" My jaw clamped down and my teeth hurt from the force of them grinding against each other. "That jerk," I hissed. Before I really knew what I was doing, I scanned the cafeteria. I knew Luke had the same lunch period. We always sat at different tables and even on different sides of the lunchroom but I knew we ate at the same time.

When I spotted him in a corner with his buddies, I untangled myself from the bench seat and started his way.

"Carrie?" E.T. called after me weakly. His voice sounded curious, yet scared. He didn't dare follow me, probably because he knew I was about to do something rash.

I must've looked like some kind of Amazon woman forging into battle, my eyes blazing with fury and my mouth set in one thin line. I marched as if I were carrying armor. It felt like I was going into war too.

I didn't care if *I'd* told my parents the same lie about Under-the-hill asking Luke to tutor me. That had been for protection: my protection and Luke's. It'd be disastrous if Mom thought Luke and I were dating. She'd have gossip spreading through town like wildfire. But why would Luke lie about it? If he didn't want his friends knowing he'd volunteered to tutor me then he shouldn't have volunteered, dang it.

He was sitting next to Pastor Curry's daughter, Liz, who was also the head cheerleader. Nathan Bates sat across from him, next to Jill Anderson, and on the other side of Jill, sat Abby. A few other football players and cheerleaders crowded in around them.

Nathan was talking when I neared the table. It sounded like he was telling some story about something that had happened to him in gym class. But I didn't hear much because when Nathan saw me looming at the end of the table glaring at Luke, his words died off. And that caused everyone to glance up, including their precious, lying quarterback.

He'd been in the middle of leaning forward to take a drink from the straw poking out of his milk carton. But when he saw me, he froze. His eyes sprang wide.

I smiled at him, a smile that probably looked anything but friendly. "I'm going to have to cancel our little meeting after school," I said.

His jaw dropped. All his friends turned to ogle him.

"But I was thinking." I tapped on my chin with one hand and set the other on my hip. "Why don't we just tell Underhill we did meet? That way I can do my thing and—" I leaned over the table, pinning him with an accusing stare. "You can still get your extra bonus points." Lifting my eyebrows, I finished, "Sound good to you?"

He opened his mouth to speak but then glanced around at the people surrounding him. When he looked back at me, he shut his mouth, apparently deciding he shouldn't say anything, and nodded.

I clasped my hands together and smiled. "Good. I'm glad we settled that, then." And I spun on my heel, leaving Luke Carter and his table of friends in my wake.

****

The phone rang five minutes after I arrived home from school. I'd just finished the apple I picked up as soon as I walked in, and was getting ready to change so I could head out to the shop.

Mom barely let the first ring settle before she swiped it off its cradle. I swore she was going to say, "Marty, is that you?" But she controlled herself enough to answer in a breathless, "Hello. Paxton residence."

I turned away and headed toward my room, tossing the apple core into the trashcan, but Mom stopped me. "Carrie. It's for you."

I was pretty sure I knew who it was before I even turned around and saw the knowing gleam in her eyes. But her wink confirmed it.

I took the phone from her and said, "Thank you." Then I pushed the disconnect button.

Mom gasped. "Carrie! How could you be so rude? What in God's name has gotten into you?"

I didn't have a chance to answer because the phone, which was still in my hand, rang again. I sighed. "I'll get it." But I wouldn't answer in front of her. I carried it to my room and shut the door on Mom's shocked face.

I pressed Talk. "Let me guess. You're sorry for lying to your friends about me and telling them Under-the-hill *forced* you into tutoring me? Am I right?"

"Carrie." His voice was a regretful sigh.

He couldn't be lying down and spread across his bed like I'd pictured him the first time he called. No, this time he was either pacing the floor, or he was seated in a straight-back wooden chair with his face buried in his hand. Out of curiosity, I almost asked him which it was. Sitting or pacing?

"You're not going to let me apologize, are you?"

"And why should I?" I said, louder than I needed to. But who could be quiet when they were spitting mad? "Who made me feel like a complete jerk yesterday for caring what other people think about money? Well, let me tell you something, Mr. Carter. Caring about financial status and caring about social status is the same dang thing."

"Carrie—"

"No!"

He had that voice—the voice that sounded humble and sorry but also like he was trying to soothe the hysterical female. It only made me madder.

"How dare you? How dare you lecture me about giving status importance and then turn around yourself and hide the fact that you volunteered to spend time with me? Let me repeat, you volunteered. If you didn't want your popular friends knowing you were tutoring a nobody then you shouldn't have volunteered."

I was breathing heavily like I'd just run a marathon. "Why *did* you volunteer, anyway?" I waited for an answer and when none came, I waited some more. I started to think he wasn't on the line anymore. "Are you still there?" I demanded.

"I'm not going to say anything until you're ready to listen to me."

I rolled my eyes. "Fine. I'm listening." I didn't plan on listening to one excuse, though.

But then he said, "You're absolutely right."

My eyebrows shot up. Of course I was right. But it was a shock to hear him admit it.

"I lied to my friends about why I was spending time with you," he said. "But it wasn't because I was ashamed of letting them know I'd volunteered to."

"Then why?"

"I thought you were going to shut up and listen for once."

"I'll listen when you have something to say."

He made a growling sound and muttered something I didn't catch, probably ran his hand through his hair too, in that harried way he had. "I lied because I didn't want anyone to know why I wanted to meet with you."

I snorted. "Well, I don't think you have to worry about that much. Because I know you volunteered and I don't have a clue as to why."

"OK, fine." I heard him sigh and I swear I could feel him struggle with himself over the phone line. "I'll tell you."

Something knocked against my chest, hard. It took me a moment to realize it was my heart. I was touched by the tone of his voice. He sounded tortured—like he had some huge mystery and I was the only human on earth able to solve it.

I wasn't going to let him know he was tugging at my heartstrings, though. No, I was rather proud of the bitter sound my voice had when I said, "Oh, so now you're going to grace me with the knowledge of your precious secret?"

"Yes," he said in a strained pitch.

"What makes you think I care what your little mystery is anymore?"

He groaned. "Carrie, let me come over. I'll explain everything."

"Why can't you tell me now?"

He sounded incredulous. "I'm not talking about it over the phone."

I hissed at him. I wanted to scream. Dang. He must have realized I'd have to know his secret—that I wouldn't rest easy until I did. I sighed. Curiosity was going to be the death of me. "OK. OK. Come over. And bring your trigonometry book. I might as well get something good out of this too."

"I'll be right over." He said it quick and didn't bother to say goodbye, merely slamming the phone down.

I wondered then if we'd ever have a phone conversation with proper farewells.

****

Luke didn't come right over like I'd expected him to. I let Mom know he was on his way and she asked if we'd worked out our problem. I told her there'd never been a problem. She only smiled to herself and rolled out dough for a pie. I leaned against the kitchen counter, resting on my elbows and snipped off a piece of the unbaked crust when she turned to fetch the pie pan. I waited there for a minute almost expecting a pounding at the door right away, even though I knew it would take him longer than that to get to my place.

But when time passed and he still hadn't shown, my smugness started to dissipate. He was going to stand me up. OK, it wasn't like a date or anything. But this was as close to a date as I'd ever come. I began to pace the living room. Mom popped her head in and asked if I wanted anything to drink. I wanted to snarl and tell her to cut the perfection act, but I only shook my head no.

When Luke finally rang the doorbell, I about tore the hinges off opening it for him. I was on the verge of asking what happened to, "I'll be right over," when I caught the look on his face. He was nervous. He looked sick-to-his-stomach pale. And his eyes darted. He held his bag down at his side today not over his shoulder and his fingers were gripped around the strap tightly enough to make his knuckles turn white. I decided against cracking a smart-aleck remark.

"Are you all right?" I asked.

He nodded but didn't speak. He was acting as if speaking would unsettle his stomach and he might vomit his after-school snack all over the floor. I shut the door behind him quietly and led him to the kitchen. Luke pulled up short when he saw my mom at the counter, pouring cherry filling into her piecrust. His gaze zipped toward me in a panic. I wanted to demand right then what the matter was.

"Hello again, Luke." Mom set her work down and smiled at him.

He nodded back but didn't return the smile. "Hi."

"Back again to tutor Carrie?" He nodded but still said nothing, and Mother smoothed her hands down the side of her apron. "Well, isn't that nice of you? Would you like something to drink?"

He raised a shoulder like he didn't care one way or the other.

"Is milk all right, then?" Mom said.

From the horror on Luke's face, I thought he might go into the whole never-consume-health-food-right-after-school spiel. But he refrained and accepted the milk with a nod.

Mom was quick to serve him, but while her back was turned Luke glanced at my pile of schoolbooks on the kitchen table. "Not here," he whispered, darting a look from my mother back to me. I wasn't about to suggest that we go to my room to study but Mom took the decision right out of my hands. She handed the milk to Luke and as he chugged it like he had cottonmouth, she glanced at the table and then to us.

"Why don't you two go to Carrie's room to study? I'm afraid I'll disturb you if you stay in here."

My jaw fell open, but Luke thanked her as he handed the empty glass back. He turned to me and almost pulled me into leading him to my room. When I glanced back, I could see my mother over his shoulder. She winked at me. Again.

I seethed the whole way. "If you say one word about my—"

"I don't care if it's decorated in pink ruffles and is stuffed with teddy bears," he said, pushing me inside. He shut the door behind us and turned. His hands were in the air as if he were ready to deliver a speech. But when he saw my room, he stopped.

"Wow. It's like stepping from day into night."

He had a point. My bed wasn't made. My clothes were strewn across the floor. I had papers and notebooks stacked in every corner. Posters I'd taped to the wall hung crookedly. I guess it was a typical teenager's bedroom but that didn't mean I was proud of it.

I glared at Luke's startled expression. "I thought you didn't care."

He shook his head. "You're right, I don't. I like your room. It's...homey."

I snorted, then jumped when he grabbed my shoulders. I looked into his eyes and my mouth fell open. I'd never seen him look so serious before.

"Swear to me," he said. "Swear that what I'm about to tell you does not leave this room."

I nodded. My heart started that odd thumping again.

"You can't tell anyone," he said.

"I won't."

He shook his head, as if not yet trusting me. "I've never said anything about any of this to anyone in my entire life."

I gasped. "You're gay, aren't you?"

His shoulders sagged and he closed his eyes. "I'm serious, Carrie."

"What?" I said. "That's exactly how you're making it sound. It's like you're coming out of the closet or something."

"I'm not gay. But that's exactly what everyone would think if they knew."

"Knew what?"

He bit his lip and stared at me. Then slowly, he turned away and bent down to his bag. He unzipped it and reached inside. I held my breath but when he pulled out a plain notebook, I exhaled like a deflated balloon. He turned back slowly.

"This," he said, and held it out. I glanced at him, asking with my eyes what it was. He didn't answer. So I reached for it. I started to tug it away from him but he had a tight grip on it.

"You swear to me, right?"

"Yes! Geez," I said, and jerked harder. He let go then and I went sprawling backward. I glared at him when I regained my balance. "What is it?"

When he refused to answer, I opened the first page.

It was filled with poems. I skimmed a few and then turned the page. There were more. I flipped through another couple of pages. All poems. I glanced at Luke. He'd fallen onto my bed and was sitting on the edge with his feet firmly placed on the carpet. He rested his elbows on his knees and his chin on his hands. His head was lowered and he was staring at the floor between his feet.

I went back to the beginning and read the first poem more carefully.

It was good. I reread it and it was even better the second time. It wasn't just good, it was really good. It wasn't that sappy junk, either, that teenagers sometimes write and then imagine they're tortured poets. This was real poetry. Being a writer, I considered myself somewhat of an expert. I wasn't good at poetry myself, but at least I could recognize a good poem when I read one.

"Who wrote these?" I said, turning the page.

Luke glanced up. "I did."

I stopped reading. *"You* wrote this?"

He nodded.

I shook my head. "I don't get it. Your secret is poems?"

He jerked to his feet then. "Never mind," he said, reaching for his notebook. But I held it away from him. He gave me a warning look. I, of course, ignored it.

"No, I guess you don't get it," he said, letting me win the notebook war. He took a huge step back, as if he needed space before he exploded. "I'm a football player. A tough guy. I'm not supposed to write sissy poetry. Everyone would think I'm gay."

"Not every male poet is gay," I said. "What about Shakespeare? Robert Frost? E. E. Cummings? Lord Byron? Now he was a real ladies' man."

"He didn't grow up in Stillburrow, either," Luke said.

I shrugged, because he was right. That would be the first assumption folks around these parts would make if they knew he leaned toward artistic pursuits.

"But it's not just that," he said. "My father expects me to go into business. To be a banker, like him."

"So be a banker," I said. "You can still write poetry on the side. That way if your work never sells, at least you have banking to fall back on."

Luke ran a hand through his hair, turned in a circle and came back to face me. "And I'm scared," he said.

My eyebrows shot up when I heard this quiet admission.

"This is important to me. I mean I really, really like doing it. And I didn't want to show it to someone and find out I'm bad. That's why I've been bugging you so much." He sat down on the bed again. When he looked up at me, his eyes were pleading and my heart fell directly at his feet.

"I didn't dare take it to a teacher. It had to be someone my age. And you're the best writer in the whole school, Carrie. You'd know if it was any good or not. Plus I've learned you're extremely honest. You wouldn't lie to me." He looked at the notebook in my hands. "So what do you think?"

Suddenly, it felt like I was holding the Holy Grail in my grasp. This was Luke Carter's heart and soul. If I told him it was bad, it would break his spirit. But could I be completely honest? I mean, I had a crush on the guy. I'd tell him I loved any piece of rubbish he wrote to make him feel better.

All right, all right, I wouldn't. I can't deny the truth. To be honest, I was suddenly jealous.

It wasn't fair. Luke Carter had the money. He had the popularity. He was already the football star. And what did I have? Writing was my only claim to fame and now he wanted that too? If anyone read these poems, they'd stop calling me "The Stillburrow Writer" and suddenly Luke would be Mr. Shakespeare himself. I couldn't tell him how good he was. But I couldn't tell him he was bad, either.

Talk about being stuck in a bad situation, huh?

And then an idea hit me. "Why don't we let the students of Stillburrow decide?"

His eyebrows crinkled in distrust. "What do you mean?"

I flipped open the notebook and scanned more poems. "Why don't we put a few sample pieces in the paper?" When his mouth opened in an instant refusal, I quickly added, "Anonymously, of course. I'll make it a survey on the editor's page. I can say that an unnamed poet would like the public's opinion on his or her work. 'Please reply with your thoughts on these poems.'"

Luke seemed to deliberate. I decided to put on a little more pressure. "I *could* tell you what I think about them. But that's just one person's point of view. What you really need, Luke, is a lot of opinions."

Luke had his hands clasped together and was holding them close to his mouth. His blue gaze was riveted toward me. "And you won't tell anyone who wrote them?"

"Cross my heart and hope to die."

He stood up, licked his lips, and then held out his hand. "We've got a deal, then."

For the second time in my life, I shook hands with Luke Carter. "I don't think you'll be disappointed," I said. "And just in case you're a big hit, we shouldn't put in your best poem first. Remember, an audience always expects a better performance the next time."

Chapter Eight

I loved the smell of newspapers hot off the press. OK, OK, by the time we got the paper back from the printing press at Paulbrook, it was cooled down. But I still loved the smell of the ink and the texture of paper under my fingers. I loved holding the first copy in my hand, and I loved the anticipation.

There was nothing like opening the cover and taking the first look at something I helped create. It was usually the bright spot of my whole week.

I also liked standing in the front hall on Friday mornings to pass out copies to students walking by. And every Friday right after school, I hand delivered the newest issue to a few old folks in town who were avid readers. My last stop on this delivery route was usually my Aunt Kay's house.

My great aunt, Kay Burke, lived in the nice section of town. Actually she lived with her nephew, my mom's brother, Uncle Stan. But when I went there, it was usually to visit Aunt Kay so I called it her house. Aunt Kay was my surrogate grandmother. She'd been the town's spinster librarian up until a few years ago when she'd fallen shelving books one evening and broken her hip. Now she was retired. But back in the day, she'd devoted her life to researching information for Stillburrow.

She had one brother and that had been Mom's dad. And since she'd never married or had kids of her own, she spoiled her brother's children. First Uncle Stan had been born. Aunt Kay had given him a $1,000 savings bond on his first birthday. And then came Andrea, my mother. But Grandma Burke died giving birth to Mom. So Aunt Kay moved in and helped her brother, Grandpa Burke, raise his two kids. She stayed with Grandpa even after Mom and Uncle Stan moved out, staying with him until he died. After Grandpa's death, she bought a little brown dachshund dog, which she named Chigger, to keep her company.

But a few years ago, about the time Aunt Kay broke her hip, Uncle Stan, who'd been living in Paulbrook with his wife and daughter, got a divorce. He'd decided to buy a house here in Stillburrow and have Aunt Kay and Chigger live with him. And every other weekend his twelve-year-old daughter, Jordan, stayed there as well.

Uncle Stan's house was huge. It was two stories high with six bedrooms, four bathrooms, a basement, and an in-ground pool in the backyard. I was envious. But then, Burke had always been a respectable name in town. Mom had really messed up when she'd hitched herself to Dad. Of course, she'd been in high school and it probably seemed exciting to date a guy seven years older than she was. I once overheard that Grandpa Burke almost disowned Mom when she came up pregnant with Marty. But Aunt Kay stepped in and smoothed down the ruffled feathers.

Still, I don't remember Mom and Grandpa ever talking when I was young. She'd always drop Marty and me off to visit and then leave. A few hours later she'd return to pick us up. We'd wobble back to the car, stuffed with Aunt Kay's snickerdoodles and ready for a nap. But after Grandpa died, Mom stayed around during our snickerdoodle visits to chat with Aunt Kay. I never thought that was odd until I got older and learned how to listen to gossip.

Anyway, Aunt Kay lived with Uncle Stan and

Chigger and sometimes Jordan. Directly across the street from her lived the president of the bank. The Carters also had a two-story house with a front circle drive. Theirs was bigger than Uncle Stan's house though, and had a three-car garage attached to it. I couldn't help but stare at it every time I went to visit Aunt Kay. I almost tripped on Uncle Stan's front porch steps I was so busy examining Luke's house.

It was a Friday afternoon. Jordan had just come to visit the weekend before so she wasn't due to show up for another seven days. I caught my footing and turned away from Luke's house, trying not to wonder if he was home.

The Central Record had published his first poem in that day's paper. Here's a clipping from my editor's column:

> It's time for the good students of Stillburrow to become literary critics. One citizen, who wishes to remain anonymous, is interested in pursuing a career in writing poetry. But our mystery poet would like to know if he or she possesses any actual talent. So let's give Anonymous our honest opinions, good or bad. Just drop off a short review of what you think of his or her work in the journalism room to let us know how you feel. And now here is a sample piece. Drum roll please:

HIBERNATION
Still deep I burrow, waiting for tomorrow.
Closed off, I bear. The open elements don't care.
Laid here in this nest, dormant now I rest,
Aching to live and roam, though still burrowed
    in my tomb.
When time brings my spring, maybe I'll rise like
    a king.

—Anonymous

I'd already received plenty of feedback to Luke's masterpiece. And just as I'd thought, they all loved him. It hurt knowing I'd lost my standing in the writing department. No one would picture me anymore when they thought of the town's writer. They would now think of this new mysterious poet.

But I was also proud. The man I had a crush on was living out his dream. He was a local star poet already. And he was destined for better things.

I knew he'd probably be looking me up any time now, eager to know what everyone thought. I was going to have fun stringing him along. I felt it was my duty to make him sweat it out as long as I possibly could before letting him see the replies. I smiled just thinking about my next round with Luke Carter.

I knocked on Aunt Kay's front door and waited. I could hear Chigger barking inside, his long toenails clicking against the hardwood floor as he came running. I couldn't resist one more peek toward the Carter House, though. I stared up at the windows and wondered which one was his room. But then Aunt Kay opened the screen door behind me and I turned back to greet her. Chigger jumped up and his paws landed on my shinbone as I stepped inside.

"My favorite grand-niece," Aunt Kay said, and immediately gave me a pillowy hug. Chigger sniffed at the brown paper bag in my hand. I lifted it out of his reach and handed it as well as a copy of *The Central Record* to Aunt Kay.

"Happy Birthday," I said.

"Oh, my goodness. Is it that time of year again?" Like a giddy child, Aunt Kay opened the bag. I tossed the paper on an end table and watched my great aunt inhale the hot air coming out of the opened sack. The aroma that spilled out of it about had Chigger going crazy. He jumped and barked, his long body flailing and twisting in the air with each bound.

"Down, boy." Aunt Kay wiggled her finger at him but she didn't close the bag. Instead, she pulled out a still-warm doughnut and took a huge bite. Her favorite food had always been glazed doughnuts. She closed her eyes and moaned as she chewed. When she opened them again to look at me, I read the thanks on her face.

"Mom will be over after her hair appointment," I said.

Aunt Kay rolled her eyes and said with her mouth full, "I swear, your daddy might've paid off his shop by now with all the money Andrea's put into fixing her hair."

I laughed because it was the truth and watched my great aunt stuff her mouth with another bite. Chigger had opted to jump on my leg and whine while staring up at me with begging eyes.

"Mom's got another gift for you. The doughnuts are from me and Marty."

Aunt Kay nodded. This time she finished her bite before saying, "And where is that boy? I don't think I've seen him since summer."

"He's…" I was trying to come up with an excuse for my brother when I realized what I was doing. Why should I make excuses for him? "He's an idiot," I finally answered. "He doesn't go to visit Mom and Dad, either. I guess he thinks he's too good for his family anymore."

"He sounds just like his mother. I heard about him moving out. And he's working at the grocery store, is it?"

"Yep." I nodded. "He looks really stupid in that little apron he's got to wear. But that hasn't stopped Abby Eggrow from giving him the goo-goo eyes."

"Eggrow? You mean the principal's girl?"

Again, I nodded. "She's the older one."

Here's where I should pause and say I never gossip...until I hit Aunt Kay's company. There's just something confidential about being around her that makes me want to spill every piece of information I know.

"He's been dating her for a few months now," I went on.

"Isn't she still in school?"

"She's a senior this year. Next year, she's going to Paulbrook for a pre-med degree. She's going to work her way up into being a doctor. The principal and his wife won't shut up about how proud of her they are. She'll be the first doctor in the family."

Aunt Kay didn't seem all that impressed. "And how is it she fell into Martin's company?"

"Well, Abby's been working at the grocery store as well. Her uncle, John Getty, gave her a job there. I guess she's going to rent some apartment off campus next semester and she wanted some money to buy furniture and that sort of stuff for it."

"I suppose her parents will be paying for her education and the apartment, then?"

I rolled my eyes. "Of course."

"I see." Aunt Kay looked down her nose at me. She disapproved of parents paying their children's way through college. She said that at age eighteen, the child was an adult and should fend for him- or herself, as she had done. And look at her, master's degree in tow, paid for by her own sweat and toil.

I knew Aunt Kay was getting ready to spill out this precise speech—about a child needing to work for his or her future, or how this was the exact thing that made our social structure so weak: children who were pampered right up into their adulthood. Blah, blah, blah. I was even braced for the speech. But Mom breezed in the front door, bearing her own gift and saving me.

Chigger quit sniffing my pant leg and dashed toward Mom. But her gift didn't smell as appetizing as mine, so the dog returned to me, whining. Mom had a new winter coat in the box she carried. Aunt Kay went to relieve her of the present before pulling her into a hug. When Aunt Kay stepped back, she eyed Mom's hair critically.

"Georgia missed a spot," she said in a snobbish tone. She dabbed at Mom's perfectly groomed head of hair and said, "I see a patch of gray."

Mom laughed good-naturedly and swatted Aunt Kay's hand away. "It's supposed to make me look distinguished."

"It makes you look old, dear."

I laughed behind my hand and quickly wiped the smirk off my face when Mom glared in my direction. That's when I decided it was time for me to leave. I hugged Aunt Kay again and she thanked me for the present. She said to thank Marty too, since it seemed I was the only member of the family who had any kind of contact with him.

"I'm sure he'll make it for Thanksgiving dinner," I heard Mom saying as I escaped out the front door. Mother would make excuses for him, of course. I didn't know why. She had no reason to lie to Aunt Kay. But she had a habit of trying to make us look perfect to everyone, even to other members of the family. I wanted to tell her she didn't have to do that with Aunt Kay, but it wouldn't have made a difference. My mother would always try to hide any imperfection she possibly could.

I was glad to be outside. I hated to sit by and listen to those two women gossip. I didn't mind talking to them separately, but together it was horror. Their continuous flow of chatter could give a person a headache.

I skipped down the front steps, my thoughts returning to my own business as I walked back home. A car passed. I didn't recognize it. In a town the size of Stillburrow, everyone knew what everyone else drove and being the daughter of the only mechanic in town, I had unique knowledge of most of Stillburrow's automobiles. But I was too busy thinking about Marty and his life to wonder about the new car or watch whose drive it pulled into. I was thinking I might mosey down to Getty's General Store and pester my brother for a while and make sure he had the latest edition of my paper.

I turned at the end of the front walk and followed the footpath toward the store. I'd just made it to the row of bushes that bordered the neighbor's yard when I heard the call.

"Carrie!"

I stopped, a little disoriented at hearing my name in this section of town. The call had come from across the street. And guess who was stepping out of the new car that had come to a stop in Carter's circle drive? Yep. It was none other than the banker's son himself.

Luke looked both ways and then jogged across the empty gravel street toward me. His eyes were a shiny blue, as if the chrome of his new bumper was reflected in them. And he was grinning, his dimple pitted as deep as it could go. His dark hair was a little windblown, like he might've been driving with the windows down. The sight made me catch my breath. Every time I looked at him, it was like seeing him for the first time. I was always struck with a fresh wave of awe.

But I managed to glance around him and peer at the Mustang. "So you finally got a new car, huh?"

It was a shocking white, waxed and shining so bright I almost had to wince to stare at it. Two black racing stripes ran up the middle of the hood and roof and back down over the trunk. It looked like he'd just driven it off a new car lot. There were fancy chrome spokes mounted in the wheels and the windows were tinted. It was a perfect fit for Luke Carter.

"Yeah, Dad gave me a loan at the bank." He seemed a little distracted and took my arm to pull me toward the bushes.

I could still see the car over his shoulder. "How old is it?"

"Two years." Luke glanced up and down the street to make sure no one was around. He had me tucked into a corner of the bushes so that if anyone happened by, we wouldn't be noticed.

"It runs pretty good, then?"

"Uh-huh," he said impatiently. "Did you hear anything about the poem today?"

I glanced up at him. He was as eager for news as I'd expected him to be. It took everything for me not to rub my hands together and grin. "Yes, I did," I said, and my gaze slid back to his ride. "How big's the engine?"

He muttered something and frowned. "Heck if I know. It's a car, OK?"

My mouth fell open. "It's a car? Is that all you can say about it? It's your car, Luke. Aren't you excited you just got a new car?"

"Yes." But he didn't sound excited. He sounded frustrated. "But I already showed it off to my friends. What I wanted to talk to you about was—"

"How fast will it go?"

"Carrie." He clenched his teeth. "Did anyone say anything to you about my poem yet?"

My eyebrows rose as if I were in shock. "So that's why you came to talk to me?" I sniffed. "I should've known that's all you'd want from me."

Luke sighed. He glanced back to his car, resigned. "I don't know how fast it'll go. I just got it, remember?"

He looked back at me like he expected me to

93

spill my guts now. Instead, I grabbed his hand and tugged. "Then let's find out."

"What?" He sounded so stunned, you'd have thought I'd just asked him to elope with me.

"Give me a ride and I'll tell you everything I know."

He didn't like the blackmail. I could tell by the way he glanced from me to the car. But it was tempting. He wanted to know what I'd heard too badly.

"I'll even duck down out of sight until we get out of town."

He began to gnaw on his lip. "It's just a car, Carrie."

"That is not just a car. It's a Mustang, a brand-spanking new Mach 1 Mustang with a V8 engine and..." Here's where I ran out of knowledge on the car. "And a lot of freaking power. Do you realize this may be the only time I'll ever get the chance to ride in a Mach 1?"

He looked at me sharply.

"Come on, Luke," I said, knowing I was getting closer to a ride. My fingers clamped around his. "It's just one ride."

Finally, he nodded. "OK. But you better have something good to tell me."

I grinned. "Oh, I heard plenty today. But what if it was all bad?"

He pulled up short. "No one liked it, did they?"

This time I laughed. "Come on, Carter. My ride's waiting." And I darted around him, taking off across the street.

"That was low," I heard him call after me. But then he started off too, racing after me.

Chapter Nine

We were both winded by the time we made it across the road to his Mustang. He came around to the passenger side with me, making my stomach do an odd little flop. He wasn't going to open my door for me, was he? But all he did was pull out his keys and unlock it. Then he stepped back.

I brushed by him as I opened the door and climbed in. "You actually lock your doors? In Stillburrow?"

He rolled his eyes. "Shut up," he said, and slammed the door in my face.

I laughed, but not for long. The smell of new car filled my nostrils. The car sat low, and spotless white leather covered everything. Even the console between the driver's and passenger's side was leather. I brushed my hand over the smooth material. Luke opened his door and slid in beside me.

When he started the engine, it purred. I sighed and rubbed my fingers along the dashboard. When I glanced over, Luke was eying me with a lifted eyebrow. All I could say was "Wow," in a reverent whisper.

He shook his head and pulled out of the drive. When we entered the street, I ducked down like I'd promised to do. My face was inches from his hand while he shifted gears. I turned away, still ducking.

"You don't have to do that," he said.

But I was busy checking out all the knobs on the

side of my seat.

"I told you I would, so I'm keeping my word." I turned one knob and the seat cranked back. "What's this do?" I asked as I pushed another button. Nothing happened for a few seconds and then I yelped. "Hey, my butt's getting hot."

Luke cracked up. He was so busy laughing he almost missed a stop sign and had to slam on the brakes to avoid sliding through an intersection. The sudden stop sent me sprawling forward and I bumped my head on his glove compartment. Thank goodness he was only going about ten miles per hour.

It still hurt, though. I glared up at Luke.

"Sorry," he said, even though amusement still lit his eyes. He glanced toward the button I'd pushed. "That's the seat warmer."

"Seat warmer?" I stared up at him. "You're kidding me."

He shook his head and didn't even try to hide his laughter this time. I narrowed my eyes at him and turned the seat warmer off. I turned my attention to the sound system. You could play a CD or plug in an MP3 player. My eyebrows rose in admiration. I found a stash of CDs in the console and began to nose through his collection of music. I pulled out one with a blond-headed guy on the cover.

"What group is this?"

When Luke checked out which CD I was holding, he gave me a strange look. "Can't you read?" When he told me the name, my eyebrows rose. I was familiar with the music because I'd heard it on the radio before.

"Really?" I said. I flipped the cover over to the back and read the names of the songs. "I always thought he spelled it 'M&M.' You know, like the candy."

Luke snorted. "You've lived in a hole your entire

life, haven't you?"

"Yes," I said, and took the CD out of the case. "Can we listen to it?"

He shrugged. "I don't care."

I looked at the stereo. "How?"

As soon as I asked the question, I bit my lip, braced for him to make fun of me again. But hey, my parents' cars only had cassette players.

Luke didn't tease, though. He pointed to a slot in the dashboard. "It's empty. Just slide it in there."

I did and waited for the music to start. When it did, I found the volume button and turned it up.

"Think it's loud enough?" he said.

"What?" I yelled back.

He grinned and so did I. When we passed the sports complex at the edge of Stillburrow, Luke nudged me. "Will you sit up already?"

I sat up, looked out the windows, staring at the fading town in the side mirror. I could feel the music reverberating through my seat. I played with the electronic buttons on the door. First I locked it and then I rolled my window down. The music rumbled out and a few cows in the pasture we were passing glanced up to watch us fly by as they munched slowly on their hay.

"Faster," I yelled, scaring the herd into running off.

Luke crinkled his eyebrows and glanced briefly at me. "Close the window. It's freezing out there."

But I only winked at him. "Wuss."

He mumbled something but I couldn't hear it over the music. The next thing I knew, he was rolling his window down too. I laughed.

"Come on, Carter. Let's see what this baby can do."

But he only shook his head. "I'm not getting a ticket on the day I bought it."

I snorted. "Yeah right." At his skeptical look, I

said, "Your best friend's the sheriff's son. What deputy would be crazy enough to ticket you? Now step on it, boy."

Finally, he took the dare and pressed his foot down. The car shot forward, and I turned the volume of the music even louder. It felt wonderful. I was so free. The breeze whirled inside and whipped my hair around. I set my face to the open wind and hollered my war cry out the window.

"You're crazy," I heard him yell.

When I risked a look at him, I saw a full grin on his face. His eyes were on the road, though. I checked how fast we were going.

"You're the one driving 115 miles per hour," I yelled back.

Then I closed my eyes and let my head fall back against the seat. I couldn't have dreamed up a better ride than this. I was sitting in a brand new sports car, with a drop-dead gorgeous guy, and the thump of bass pulsating through my chest. And I thought, maybe I can't have Luke Carter, but I'll always have this moment.

I don't know how long I had my eyes closed but I think I drifted off for a few seconds. I came to when Luke slowed and pulled the car into a drive lined with trees on each side. I glanced around, realizing we were by the lake. The Lake was what Stillburrow called the large man-made pond that Old Man Roper had willed to the city. He'd owned the pond and hundreds of acres of farmland around it but had no family left to inherit anything. So Stillburrow took over maintenance on the place and labeled it our city lake. And Luke had just turned into the road that led to the camping ground, which was the major make-out spot for all Stillburrow teens.

I sat up. "What're you doing?"

"I don't think anyone will be here at this time of day," Luke said. He must have seen the sudden unease in my eyes. "Relax. I just didn't know where else to go."

I leaned over and turned the radio down. "It looks kind of creepy this time of year." All the trees were bare except for a few dead brown leaves still clinging to branches. It was much prettier in the summer when everything was green and in bloom.

Rubbing the goose bumps on my arms, I rolled up my window and heard Luke chuckle. I told him to shut up, but that only increased the volume of his laugh. We followed the curving road until the opening of the camping ground came into view. I sat forward when I caught sight of blue through the trees.

"Hey, someone *is* here," I said. I leaned forward, straining to see. Luke slowed down. And then I gasped. "That's Marty's truck." I ducked down just as Luke entered the clearing.

I heard Luke snicker. "Now who doesn't want to be seen with whom?"

I gave him a dirty look and was about to tell him to shut up again when I saw his eyes go wide and his mouth drop open.

"What?" I started to sit up, but suddenly Luke's hand shot out and pushed my head back down.

"Nothing."

"What is it?" I said. This time, my voice was frantic. Something had happened to Marty. I struggled to sit up.

"Dang it, Carrie," Luke said, trying to spin the car in a circle with one hand and hold my head with the other. "Stay down."

"What's wrong with my brother?" I snarled, batting at his hand.

I saw a glimpse of Luke's face then. He flushed and lit into a half grin. "Nothing's *wrong* with him. He seemed to be doing fine to me."

I stared at his face. Luke had us turned around

now and I saw the tree-tops lining our path again. We were heading back out of the camping ground. And that's when I realized what was going on. His hand loosened in my hair and I immediately sat up, glaring at him as I shoved my bangs out of my eyes.

"He was out there with someone, wasn't he?"

Luke's silence was admission enough.

"It was Abby," I said, already knowing the truth.

Luke gave a slight nod of the head. We turned away from the camping ground and I looked back, though I couldn't see anything now.

"What'd you see?" I needed to know.

"A lot more than I wanted to," he said with a snort.

I stared at his face. He shifted in his seat as if he were uncomfortable. I turned back around to face the front and folded my arms over my chest. "That idiot."

"Marty?" Luke glanced at me. "Why do you say that?"

"He's going to get hurt," I whispered.

The car slowed and pulled down a different country road. Luke parked to the side by a row of trees and killed the engine. The music that had filled the interior died, and silence spilled in around us. When he turned to me, he said softly, "You really care about him, don't you?"

I couldn't look at him. I stared at the road that stretched ahead of us. It seemed to go on forever. "He's my brother," I finally said.

I felt warm fingers touch the back of my hand. "Don't worry about him so much. Abby's a nice girl."

I spun toward him then. I could feel the heat rise in my face. "Oh, I'm sure she is. She's perfectly nice for someone like you."

His mouth fell open in surprise. "What's that supposed to mean?"

"I mean, it's fine for her to date someone like

you or one of your friends. Her mom and dad would compliment her for her choice in boyfriends. But not my brother. I guarantee you the principal and his wife don't know anything about them being together. I guarantee you that would be the end of Abby's little fling if her parents did know. And yes, I know it's a fling," I said, when I saw Luke's mouth open as if to argue.

"I heard Abby's sister, Sidney, talking to her friends in the girls' bathroom at school," I continued. "I heard her say Abby thought she was so cool to date an older guy. But it's not going to stop her from going off to college next year and leaving him behind."

Luke shook his head. "And how do you know it's not just a...what'd you call it...a *fling* for your brother too?"

"Because Marty's never spent so long with one girl before."

I didn't know how to make Luke understand but I suddenly wanted to. "I think he moved out because of her." I turned to stare out the passenger-side window as I said it, because it seemed too personal to admit to Luke's face. "I found out he was seeing her right after he packed up and rented that place with Austin Fitz. I think he wanted to show her he wasn't a loser. To impress her, you know?" When I glanced over at Luke, I was startled at the intensity with which he stared at me. "Next year, she's going to run off and find some college stud and Marty's going to be left here alone."

"You don't know what's going to happen." He took my hand and looked deep into my eyes. "Paulbrook isn't that far away. Abby could come back to visit him every weekend."

"Why would she want to?" I yanked my hand away. "She'll be a fancy city girl by then, and Marty will still be a small town guy that works at a grocery store." I sighed and stared out the window again. I couldn't look at Luke. "She's going to make a laughingstock out of him."

"Carrie, I think Marty can take care of himself. He knows what he's getting into."

I didn't want to say it wasn't as much Marty I was worried about, as it was me. Being with Luke was what I wanted more than anything. And that had even less promise than thinking Marty and Abby would end up happily ever after. I didn't want to go back to town where Luke was the cool guy and I was best friends with the school dork. Where he hung out with cheerleaders and football players and I stayed home every evening and either read or wrote.

I wanted to be like other girls. I wanted to understand why they put on so much makeup and worried about clothes. I wanted to have lots of friends, talk on the phone for hours, and gossip about who liked who. I wanted to care about stupid stuff like that. I wanted to be normal.

No, that's not quite right. I liked being who I was. I liked being editor of the paper and focusing so much of my attention on that. I just didn't want to feel so odd anymore. I didn't want to be ashamed to be a grease monkey's daughter.

I wanted to stay right here, in this new car where it was just Luke and me. I wanted to stay me, but I wanted Luke to stop being the macho guy he was in school, and be the poet who was shy about his abilities and liked to argue and debate everything with me. This was my Luke. And I didn't want him to go away like I knew he would.

But who was I kidding?

"You're right," I said, feeling miserable. "Marty can take care of himself."

I turned to stare out the passenger-side window, focusing on an old house that had been abandoned for as long as I could remember. I said, "They really ought to tear that place down. Just look at that sagging roof."

Luke gave a soft laugh behind me. "That would involve change."

"What do you mean?"

"Haven't you ever noticed this town's stuck in a time capsule? It's like we've never heard of the term progress. I mean, there's hardly any cell phone towers around and forget about high speed internet."

"High speed what?" I asked, glancing back to give him a puzzled look.

He opened his mouth to explain, when it dawned on him I was joking. "You always have to be a smart-aleck, don't you?"

We shared a smile.

I looked into his face and relished these minutes where I could ogle him selfishly. I knew I should give him the information he wanted from me now, but I could only stare. It took me a moment to notice his expression, though.

His gaze had been roaming my face but had paused on my left ear. When he snorted out a surprised laugh, I frowned.

He pointed a finger toward my hair. "Uh, I think the wind messed it up some."

I patted my head, my face flaming.

"Here," Luke said, and flipped down his visor, lighting up the mirror underneath. I looked up and groaned. Not only had the wind caught a hold of my hair and ripped it half out of its ponytail, it had also knotted and twisted it into a healthy-sized rat's nest.

I tried to ignore the fact that Luke was sitting next to me—and already knew exactly what the disaster looked like—and ripped the holder out of my hair. I combed through the mess with my fingers but there were knots everywhere. When I caught him staring again, I glared.

"What?" I demanded. But he continued to gawk. I patted at my hair and wondered what he could possibly be thinking about the mess.

"I've never seen it all down before," he said.

Startled, I glanced back in the mirror. I'd seen it down millions of times. I just didn't leave the house with it loose. There was too much of it to let it run wild. I tried to see it how Luke must see it. It was curly—so curly it bobbed. Tight little curls framed my face like a border full of personality. From the corner of my eye, I saw Luke lift his hand toward one spiraling lock.

But when I turned to him, he lowered his fingers and shifted his attention out the window. I stared at his profile for a second, breathing hard.

"It's pretty," he said, more to the windshield than to me.

I wanted him to lift his hand again. I wanted him to touch my hair.

"I think yours is prettier."

He laughed. "Guys do not have pretty hair."

"Well, yours is."

I reached over and touched his hair. I thought maybe if I touched his, he might get the guts to touch mine. But at contact, I gasped.

"It's so soft."

I ran my fingers through the part that always curled around a cowlick when it got wet. I scooted over, leaning across the console between us.

"Carrie."

His voice sounded strained so I looked down. I hadn't realized I'd moved so close. But when I gazed into his face, we were only a breath apart. I was positioned a little above him so I could reach his hair. He lifted his face up to stare at me. His eyes were a blazing blue.

That's when he touched my hair. He drew his fingers through the curls to cup my head. Then he tilted his chin to the side and pulled me down. I was shocked when our mouths connected. He was kissing me.

Oh my God, Luke Carter was kissing me.

I didn't even think to close my eyes. Of all the times I'd imagined my first kiss, I never thought it would take me by surprise like this.

I stared at his face for a second, unable to move. And then I realized that maybe I should participate a little. I felt my lips soften and my lids slide shut. My hand rested on the side of his neck, and I kissed him back...and felt it all the way to my toes.

At that moment, I discovered where all of my erogenous zones were because they all became inflamed. It was like a tingle but with a hundred times the voltage. Luke's mouth slid sideways where his lips could be more accommodating. My ears buzzed. I thought I might blow a fuse with all the wattage flowing through my veins. When his tongue entered my mouth, I jerked back.

I don't know why I did. I hadn't wanted to put a stop to the kiss. This was my big moment. I was steaming up the windows with Luke Carter. But the shock of his tongue had knocked me flat. I hadn't been prepared at all. Not that it was bad. It was wet and warm and would have ended as the best kiss I was sure I'd ever have. Yes, it had been great, right until I'd messed up and jerked away.

I scuttled back to the passenger's side, banging my elbow on the gearshift as I fled. I still couldn't believe I'd pulled away from him. Pressing my back against the seat, I stared out the front window at the horizon, feeling like the loser I was.

The day was turning to dusk and the sunset was spread before me in a fierce glowing-orange-and-pink masterpiece. I wanted to soak into its wonder and appreciate the full beauty of that descending sun, but my throat was closing and my heart was sprinting, making my breathing, and in effect all thinking, too difficult to manage at the moment.

I wondered what was going on inside Luke. What did he think of me? I'd started this by touching his hair and practically crawling into his lap. What other way could a healthy teenage boy react? It wasn't me—it was just the situation that had prompted his actions. Right?

I wanted to glance over and see how he was responding, just peek at his face. My eyes burned as I focused on seeing him out of my peripheral vision. I couldn't chance the thought that Luke could possibly be interested in me, Carrie Paxton. He'd just met up with a moment of insanity and...and kissed me. That's all.

"I'm sorry," he said, his voice filled with a coarse regret.

See, he hadn't meant to do it at all. But with my doubts confirmed, tears smeared my vision and the sunset blurred. I nodded.

I wanted to say, "I'm sorry," too. "I'm sorry I pulled away. So come back here and finish what you started." But I couldn't say that. A thick silence stretched across the interior of the car and filled it like a deadly vapor, almost smothering us to death.

Luke sighed. It was a long, solemn sigh I felt all the way to the pit of my stomach. I saw his arms reach out and rest on the top of the steering wheel. Behind us, a car passed on the dirt road leading back to Stillburrow. I looked back just in time to see the blue truck hurry by.

"That was Marty's truck," I said. I pressed my hands deep into my lap.

"I saw."

I glanced over at Luke then. His hair was still mussed from where I'd touched it. My fingers started to tingle, remembering the texture of each silken strand.

"I guess they're finished, huh?"

"I guess." Luke closed his eyes and rested his head on the backrest. I saw him swallow.

"Maybe you should take me home now."

I said it timidly, but by the way it had Luke's head coming off the rest and his blue eyes narrowing at me, you would have thought I'd shouted it.

"What are we doing, Carrie?" he whispered— almost hissed.

I shrugged. It seemed useless to point out that of the two of us, I had the least experience in this department. But Luke seemed to realize it soon enough and turned his head away with a bitter laugh. He leaned forward, set his feet on the clutch and the brake and turned the ignition.

The car came to life, roaring under us. Luke stayed leaning forward. His head bowed a little as if he was straining to rest his cheek on the steering wheel. "Your parents are probably wondering where you are."

All I could do was shrug. "They won't be worried yet. I'll just tell them I was at the library."

He turned toward me with a probing stare. "You don't want them to know you were with me?"

I made a face by squinting my eyes, silently saying, *Heck no, I'm not telling them.* "It'd just make them think we were dating or something."

"What if—" He stopped talking so abruptly I had to probe further.

"What if what?"

He shook his head and slid the car into first. "Nothing."

"What?" I insisted.

He lifted a hand to stop me. "I said it was nothing."

I zipped my mouth shut. I wanted to ask what his problem was but I was sure I already knew. He was mad at himself for kissing me. I stared out the side window and acted like I was pushing the hair out of my face when I was actually rubbing the moisture out of the corner of my eye with my palm.

We took the country roads back to town. When we hit the city limits, I tried to duck down. But after a sharp, "Don't," from Luke I pulled myself back up. The windows were tinted anyway. No one would see me. Probably.

"You can drop me off here," I said, as we approached the corner where he could turn to head home. Luke only shot me a dirty look, at which I slumped down saying, "Or not."

If he'd been a cartoon character, steam would've been rolling from his ears. I'd never seen him so ticked. When he pulled to a stop in front of my house, he didn't look at me.

"So," he said. "See you at school."

My throat was jammed up so I could only nod. I grabbed the door handle, then remembered the whole purpose of our ride. "Oh! I almost forgot."

I reached into the pocket of my jeans and pulled out a lump of folded paper. Luke glanced over. When I tossed it into his lap, he frowned at me and cautiously picked up the bundle.

"That's all the feedback I received from putting your poem in the paper."

Luke had been in the process of unfolding the stack of papers but when he heard what it was, he stopped. "You were carrying it around in your pocket?"

I nodded and tried to smile, but failed miserably. "Somehow, I had this feeling you'd jump me from out of nowhere and demand to know what everyone thought."

His eyes moved to the sheets still folded in his fingers. "Did a lot of people reply, then?" He slowly moved his fingers over the still-folded sheets.

I took the papers gently from his hands. "It's the

biggest response since I wrote an editorial about getting a fire station built in town." I unfolded the notes and Luke's gaze suddenly strayed. He couldn't look at the results, so I said, "They loved you."

He came back. "Really?"

I grinned, a true grin this time, at his expression of complete disbelief. He snatched the papers out of my hand and read through each comment. His face moved from incredulous to ill to ecstatic in only moments. Then he crushed the comments in his fist and looked at me.

"They really did like it," he whispered.

I bit my lip. "I know."

"They liked me, Carrie." I think he had to repeat the words to believe them. And when it soaked in, he suddenly looked like he could grab me and pull me toward him to wrap his arms around me and bury his face in my hair. But then he looked down at the stack of replies without touching me.

"This can't be real." He slapped the critiques gently against his thigh and turned to me. "Thank you," he said quietly.

Chapter Ten

It was after that first kiss I decided to start keeping a diary—this very book, in fact. I called it a journal, though, since I thought diaries were for sissy girls who only wrote about what boy they had a crush on that week. I didn't plan on writing just about my crush alone. Yeah, that was probably the biggest reason I wanted one but it seemed that so many things were changing around me. I knew I would look back on this year one day and try to remember the exact smells and the exact color of things I was currently experiencing. And I knew they were things I didn't want to forget.

I know, I know. I should've already started a journal by that point. Sixteen, almost seventeen, seemed old for someone like me to begin such a task. But I never thought I had an exciting life...not until Luke Carter deemed me interesting enough to kiss.

So I decided I needed a notebook. Yes, I spent most of my time writing and had plenty of notebooks. But I wanted a new one, something fresh and clean that had never been written in before. I knew there was no way I'd find one in my room. I wrote so much every notebook I owned was already half filled with scribbles.

So I decided to ransack Marty's old room. I don't think I ever saw him do over an hour's worth of homework so I knew he had to have dozens of brand new, spotless notebooks.

His room was half empty. His clothes, posters,

and even the pillows off his bed were gone. But other things remained.

He'd actually won first place at the science fair one year. He'd invented a new kind of water bomb and his demonstration of it had been outstanding. His trophy for that was still sitting on his dresser along with some loose change from which I pocketed the quarters and dimes.

I started searching under his bed. Marty kept old school things there like yearbooks and past report cards. Mom had everything stored in a Rubbermaid container. I shimmied down on my hands and knees and reached for the box. The dust almost choked me when I pulled it out. And I knew then that Mom had kept his room sacred, not stepping foot into his personal domain since he'd left.

Waving away the dust cloud so I could see, I opened the box and sorted through it. It smelled musty and stale.

I found a picture he'd drawn when he was in kindergarten. The paper was yellowed and ragged at the corners. The drawing showed Mom and Dad and Marty standing in a row and holding hands. Mom had a fat stomach so she must've been pregnant with me. At the top, in the worst handwriting I'd ever seen, Marty had written, "I love Mommy. I love Daddy. I love baby."

I sighed. Too bad Marty hadn't stayed that sweet over the years.

I shoved the drawing back into the pile and sifted some more. No notebook. Growing more and more restless, I pushed the box back under the bed and stood up, wiping my knees with my hands.

The closet was the next place to look. I pulled the string for the light and once again a dust cloud enveloped me. It made the confining closet look dim and hazy.

I had to stand on tiptoes to peek at the top shelf. As I did, I bumped into some clothes still hanging there. It rustled up a smell I associated with my brother. And for the briefest of moments I missed him. That was something I would never tell a living soul. But the smell of Marty reminded me of when we were younger and he would sometimes let me ride in the front seat when we went with Dad to test drive a car. And it reminded me of when we went grasshopper hunting together. Marty let me hold the jar while he caught the grasshoppers, which was fine with me because I had no desire to touch the creepy-crawly critters. But it had made me feel important to hold that jar for my big brother. Of course, then Marty would torture the poor thing by pulling its legs off one by one, and I'd go running to Mom, bawling. But standing there, in his closet, made me miss those old days.

It also reminded me of how so many things had changed. Marty had moved out, and someday I would too. We weren't foolish little kids anymore, pulling off grasshopper legs. I sighed. It was almost depressing to think about growing up.

But then I spotted what looked like a notebook stuck under a shoebox. More determined than ever to preserve my memories of fair youth, I shoved the clothes aside and peered over them to get a look at what was on his closet shelf. Sure enough, there was a plain, three-holed notebook wedged under everything.

I tugged on it, trying to shimmy it out from under the shoebox. But when I pulled it free the shoebox came as well. My fingers clamped desperately around the notebook as the contents of the box that had been on top of it spilled out and onto me. I ducked, wrapping my hands over my head to cushion the blow. Objects fell around me, bumping and scraping against my arms and fingers before crashing in a heap at my feet. The notebook had acted as an umbrella throughout the ordeal, protecting my noggin from harm.

I stood there, half paralyzed for a second, until everything settled on the carpet. Then I checked myself for damages. I fared the collision OK. There were a few stinging scrapes on my arms, but the skin wasn't bleeding or broken.

I looked at the floor. The shoebox, empty now, lay propped against my shoe, and old fireworks littered the floor around my feet. I bent down and picked up a bundle of sparklers and a string of cracker jacks fell from my hair, landing on a stick of roman candles.

For a moment, I could only stare. There were fireworks everywhere.

I wondered how old they were and if they were still good. Marty loved the Fourth of July. It was the only time of year he didn't get into trouble for blowing something up. And he always went crazy buying every kind of firework he could find. I swear he used to save his money all year just for the Fourth of July. I had to admit I loved the season too. I don't think I had one bad memory of Independence Day. Maybe it was the hot summer sun, the smell of freshly cut grass, the taste of homemade ice cream, or the fact that I didn't have to worry about school. It was just one of those holidays where nothing went wrong.

I started to pick everything up, thinking of one year when just Mom, Dad, Marty and I drove out into the country and celebrated the Fourth. Mom packed a picnic and Dad spread out an old blanket for us all to sit on. I'd never seen Marty have so much fun entertaining us with his fireworks display. I settled on Mom's lap and tried hard to stay awake and see every explosion. I wanted to keep the night alive because I never remembered my mom smiling so much. She never let me sit on her lap during church when I got tired. She used to say it made the family look like bunch of monkeys crawling on each other. So I would just inch past her and settle myself on Dad's lap. But that night, where no one else could see us, I was allowed to curl myself into her lap. She ran her hands through my hair, and her laughter vibrated through me like a soothing rocking chair. And it cradled me right to sleep. When I woke up the morning after, I thought it had all been a dream: a sweet, lovely dream.

I set the last bottle rocket in the shoebox and stood up. I was sliding the box back onto the shelf when the idea hit me. That Fourth of July had been the exact kind of memory I wanted to put in my journal. I paused in my task, thinking about it, already planning. The memory was so fresh in my mind I swore I could still taste the watermelon we'd eaten that night.

It had to be written about. It had to be immortalized and kept precious forever in words— beautiful, flowing words.

And with that thought, I made up my mind.

When I left Marty's room, I had the notebook plus a shoebox full of fireworks tucked under my arm. And I had a plan in my head. It seemed like such a good idea, I acted before I even thought it completely through.

I tossed the box on my bed as soon as I hit my room and I instantly looked up Luke's phone number. It wasn't until after I dialed that I panicked. I started to think about the flaws in my plan. What was I doing, involving Luke Carter in my idea? I'd never even called him before. And we hadn't exactly been on the best of terms lately.

Since the kiss in his car, we'd ignored each other in school and he hadn't come over to tutor me. Not that I felt I needed tutoring anymore. I actually understood what Under-the-hill was teaching in class these days and I knew I was doing better. But the situation between Luke and me was ridiculous. We acted as if we were complete strangers, as if we'd never talked to each other, as if he'd never come to my home and showed me how to make a true after-school snack, as if he'd never kissed me.

There was one time at lunch when I'd glanced up and caught him staring at me from across the cafeteria. I paused and stared back because his look puzzled me. He was scowling, yet he didn't look mad. He looked...I don't know, like he was disappointed or something. And then his friend, Nathan, caught him and turned to see whom Luke was watching. When Nathan saw me, he said something to Luke I couldn't hear. Luke looked away then and shook his head. His lips barely moved as he gave Nathan some kind of reply. I had no idea what Luke's response was, but it had Nathan turning back to gape at me. He pointed a finger in my direction and it looked like he said, "Her? Are you sure?" And Luke only nodded with his head bent low.

I was still thinking about that when the first ring echoed in my ear. My hand started to shake. What was I doing? I'd gotten some stupid idea after seeing those fireworks and now I was acting before thinking. I had no idea what I was going to say to him when he answered. And what if his mom or dad picked up? I knew I wasn't ready to talk to a Carter parent yet, so I decided to disconnect.

But then Luke's voice said, "Hello?"

I couldn't speak at first. My heart was thumping too madly and I had to calm myself. Luke said hello again. And I bit my lip after taking a huge lungful of air.

"Hey, Lucas," I said.

He paused and I swore it was to check his caller ID. Then he said, "Carrie?" He sucked in a breath.

"What're you doing?" If the bewilderment I heard in his voice was genuine, the boy was clueless. I could almost see him glancing out his window to check if the sky had turned orange and the ground was purple.

"Hello?" he said again. "Carrie?"

My heart leapt. A battle inside me began. I was tempted to hang up and forget about my crazy scheme. But I wanted to see him again. I didn't want to make a fool of myself over him, but I hadn't shaken off my impulsive frame of mind yet.

"I'm still here," I said, and sat down on the corner of my unmade bed.

He waited for me to go on but when I said nothing, he hesitantly asked, "Do you need some help with trig?"

I shook my head, though he couldn't see it. "No," I said.

"OK." I could picture him shaking his own head, trying to clear it. "Then...what's going on?"

I gulped in a lungful of air. "Could you meet me tonight on the corner of Oak and Adams with your car?" He lived near there and Oak Street trailed off into the country toward the lake. We could drive out somewhere and set off the fireworks.

"Why?" I heard him say.

"I'll let you know when we get there." My stomach was churning. What was I doing? He was going to say no. Of course, he was going to say no. "How about seven," I said. "It'll be dark by then, right?"

"Uh..." Luke let out an uncertain laugh. "What's this all about?"

I fell back onto the mattress and stared up at my ceiling. I suddenly wanted to say, "Never mind. I didn't mean to call." But instead I said, "It's about our little secret."

"Our—" His voice cut out, then he said so quietly

I could barely hear him. "More people wrote in to the paper?"

"No."

"Then what?"

I grinned. If I wasn't good at anything else, I was great at frustrating the poor guy. "Meet me and you'll find out."

Luke took forever to decide, but finally he relented. My chest began to swell. We were going to meet again. I was going to see Luke alone one more time.

For the first time, we said goodbye to each other before hanging up.

****

"Since I'm the one driving, don't you think you better tell me where we're going now?"

I shut the passenger door of Luke's Mustang and glanced over at him. He darted a suspicious peek at my book bag. It was stuffed full, and lumpy. But he didn't ask what was inside, probably because he knew I wouldn't tell him.

I shrugged. I was nervous. I hadn't yet fully decided if this was a good idea or not, therefore I hadn't settled on all the details of my plan, like where this event would take place.

"It doesn't matter where we go," I answered. "As long as it's outside of town where we're alone."

Luke glanced at the bag again as I slid it to the floorboard between my knees. He put the car into gear. "You're not one of those serial killers that gets her victims alone and then slices them open and drinks their blood, are you?"

I wiggled my eyebrows. "What's your blood type?"

He laughed and ran a hand through his hair. Then he mumbled something under his breath. It sounded like he said, "I can't believe I'm doing this."

"We can always go back," I said, watching him,

almost hoping he'd stop and turn around but wanting him to keep going at the same time.

"Heck no," he said. "There's no calling it quits now. I've got to see what this is all about."

He pulled the car off onto another country road and came to a halt. He killed the engine but kept the headlights on. When I realized where we were, I gasped softly. It was our spot. I turned to him, ready for an explanation.

He shrugged, looking a little embarrassed. "I didn't know where else to go."

My insides grew warm and snuggly. Instantly, I thought of our last visit to this exact spot. I felt like we were repeating history, returning to our first kiss. It was like Luke and I were destined to repeat the scene until we got it right.

"All right," he said, turning to me. "What's in the bag?"

I rolled my eyes. "I'm glad to see you too," I said, and reached forward to lug the bag onto my lap. I unzipped it and moved it back when Luke leaned over to peek inside. He glanced up and I shook my finger at him.

"To start with," I said, trying to sound dramatic, "we have this." I pulled the first item free. It was a thick red-and-white-checkered tablecloth.

In the dark, I caught a glimpse of Luke arching one eyebrow. He lifted the tablecloth out of my hand. "A blanket?" He sounded baffled.

I nodded. "Very good. Now be a doll, will you, and spread that out on the ground."

His head swiveled up to me. "On the ground? Outside?"

I nodded. And he shook his head.

"You've got to be kidding me. It's freezing out there."

"Well then, you're in luck because I've got something to warm us up." I pulled out a full bottle of wine. He snatched that away from me too, peering at the label. When he saw it was the same bottle he'd pulled from my mom's kitchen drawer, I added, "Be glad I decided against the ice cream."

He looked up, shaking his head. "You never cease to surprise me."

I took the blanket back and handed him a silver utensil. "I also thought to bring a corkscrew. There's no cups, though."

"So where's the food?" He smiled as he worked the corkscrew into the cork. When I pulled out the Tupperware container, his smile dropped and his jaw fell open.

"Right here," I said, grinning. "But it's not much." The plastic was fogged from the temperature difference inside the container. Luke bent down to peek inside.

"What is it?"

I popped the lid. "Cheese, apples, rolls, and…watermelon," I said proudly, showing off the ruby-red, bite-sized chunks inside. "They don't sell whole watermelons at Getty's General this time of year. But I found this much being sold with a whole fruit platter of grapes, pineapple chunks and melon balls."

"Why watermelon?" he said.

"I'm trying to re-create something," I said. I rested the bag in my lap, the last surprise still inside. "Tell me what red-and-white-checkered tablecloths, wine, and watermelon remind you of."

"Um…" He frowned as he tugged harder on the corkscrew. Then he said, "Summer, I guess," just as the cork popped out. The bottle teetered and some juices dribbled down the side of his finger. He licked the droplets off. My stomach dropped as I watched his tongue lap up the excess. He glanced over at me, seeming unaware of how much I'd been gawking. "It reminds me of summertime and picnics."

I reached inside the bag, wanting more than anything to impress him. "You're getting close," I said, and came up with a fistful of the fireworks I'd nabbed. I waved them back and forth like a flag. "Now what does it remind you of?"

Luke took a wad of sparklers out of my hand and stared at them as if he'd never seen them before. "The Fourth of July," he said, his voice full of awe.

"Ever celebrated the Fourth in November?"

He shook his head. "I think I'm about to, though."

I grinned, opened my door and got out of the car. I could hear him still inside, groaning and muttering about the temperature before I shut him in. Finally he got out too, carrying the opened bottle.

It was freezing. There was a bit of a wind too, which made matters worse. I pulled the collar of my coat up over my neck and huddled deep inside. I watched Luke's silhouette as he passed the headlights. The lights caught him perfectly. He shivered and rubbed his arms.

"How'd you talk me into doing this again?"

I set the tablecloth, fireworks and watermelon on the hood of his Mustang. When I looked up at him, I knew my cheeks and nose were red with cold.

"I want you to write a poem about this," I said.

Luke glanced around him at the night. He rubbed his arms and a cloud of white fog exited his mouth. "About what?"

I nodded toward the hood where my supplies lay strewn like an Independence Day hood ornament. "About all that."

"The Fourth of July?"

I grinned at his bewildered tone. "That's why I planned this. I love the Fourth of July...the lights, the food, the festivities. And I want words to describe how it always makes me feel. Only...I can't write like that. Not like you can." I looked up and caught a side view of his face as he studied the tablecloth. I saw that overbite of his and my stomach dropped.

For moment, he said nothing. Then he whispered, "OK."

The air rushed out of my lungs. I hadn't realized I'd been holding my breath, waiting for his response. I hadn't realized his answer would be so important either, until he'd given it and I felt the relief. Suddenly, I wanted to hug him and thank him profusely. But then I caught myself.

I twisted my body away so he couldn't see my face and I reached for the cloth. I was about to lay it out on the ground in front of the headlights, but he stopped me by quietly taking the blanket from my hands. Without a word, he went out in front of the car a few feet and flipped the tablecloth up in the air. For a moment, the cloth fluttered in the cool night and wavered above him. As it began to float down, Luke stepped back and held the blanket wide. It landed perfectly, settling over gravel and dirt with such grace and style my breath caught in my chest. Luke's back was to me as he bent down to straighten a slightly wrinkled corner. His shoulders were wide and well formed. And I saw his midnight hair glistening in the headlights.

He stood slowly and I noticed his grace of movement. He was so beautiful. As a chilly gust of wind came up and stirred his hair and clothing, artistically ruffling his perfection, it seemed like he was meant to look exactly as he was.

When he turned, I swallowed and held up a watermelon piece. He stared at it a moment before reaching out slowly and taking it from my fingers. My stomach curled as he lifted it to his mouth and took it between his teeth.

"Mmm," he said. "At least it still tastes sweet this time of year."

I tried my own sample bite, and while I chewed Luke led me to the tablecloth and we sat down. It was cold enough to make my teeth rattle, but they didn't because the temperature didn't bother me. In fact, a strange warmth had ignited in my stomach and was steadily working its way up my arms and down my legs. And the closer Luke settled himself next to me, the hotter it burned.

Chapter Eleven

We taste-tested the wine first. Luke held the bottle by the neck as he drank and I watched his throat work when he swallowed. He wiped his mouth with the back of his hand. His blue eyes were bright as they met mine. Then he moved his hand from his face and sighed. After he handed the drink to me, he never took it back. I hadn't had more than one glass before. And when I told Luke this, he said I wouldn't get as sick if I drank slowly.

It was so nice being there with him. I forgot I'd been nervous, and I teased him about the way he sucked the juice out of his watermelon before eating it.

After we polished off the rest of our snack—which he just had to note was all "health" food—we delved into the fireworks. I realized I hadn't brought any form of fire. But Luke came up with the idea of using his car's cigarette lighter to light the bamboo punk I discovered mixed in with the fireworks.

We set off the jumping jacks first. They made little sparks of light and sounded like crackling pops in the night. Then we worked our way through the sparklers. I tried to spell my name but Luke started to use his as a sword and we ended up having a jousting match instead—a short one because the sparklers stayed lit for only so long.

Next we set off bottle rockets. We'd toss them in the air right before they took off. Luke had better aim than I did because mine would dive right into the grass before popping. His always managed to fly up and explode into a short volley of crackles, briefly lighting the night.

We collapsed on the tablecloth when every last firework had been set off. I was surprised there'd only been a few duds in the old pack. Almost everything had exploded with a satisfying report.

I sat huddled in my coat, shivering, my teeth chattering uncontrollably.

From his corner of the blanket, Luke glanced up. "Cold?"

I sent him a get-real look. "Nope. I'm nice and toasty."

He sighed. "You really can't control that smart mouth, can you?"

"Would you rather I had a stupid mouth?" I watched him as I tilted the bottle up and took a long drink. When I was done, I started to shiver again.

"Come here," Luke said.

I scooted away and gave him an uneasy look.

He rolled his eyes. "Are you telling me you can invite me out here to the middle of nowhere all alone in the dark of the night, but you're too chicken to sit next to me and share a little body heat?"

I stared at the headlights of his car, wondering how much longer they could stay on before the battery went dead. I trembled again and used my numbed fingers to wipe the hair out of my eyes. "It's not the middle of nowhere," I said. "We're not that far from town."

Luke took two handfuls of my coat and yanked me across the blanket toward him. His voice nearly growled as he said, "Get over here before you freeze to death."

"What a polite invitation," I said, trying not to fall into him as he threw off my balance.

But he ignored my sarcasm. "Geez," he said, rubbing my coat between his fingers. "This thing's paper thin."

"That's because I can't afford something decent," I said sarcastically, a little put off that he'd made fun of my favorite jacket.

"Well, being the rich guy I am, I can," Luke shot back and pulled open his coat to wrap it around us both. He propped my back against his chest and cradled me in a warm embrace. Then pulling the edge of the tablecloth over our laps, he cuddled in close. I held in a dreamy sigh and looked up at the stars while resting my head back against him. The breeze froze my toes and the ground was hard under me but I was toasty everywhere else.

Luke tried to give me another drink of the wine, but some spilled out and leaked down my chin. He wiped the juice away with his thumb. His warm breath was at my ear and his lips were close to my jaw when he murmured, "Thank you for tonight."

I felt his hand in my hair then, working the clasp from my ponytail. "Be careful," I said, closing my eyes. "If you get too close, you might slip and fall for me."

I'm not sure why I said it. I was trying to joke, but it wasn't so funny. Luke pulled my hair the rest of the way free. Fingers skimmed over my cheek and then against my scalp. It felt like I was sitting with my back to a campfire, he was so warm.

"Maybe I already have," he said.

My mouth fell open. I jerked away and twisted my body around to face him. "No, you haven't." I made it sound more like a demand than a denial.

Luke sat up and the red-and-white-checkered patterns slid off his knee. He demanded right back, "Why can't I?"

I dug a finger into my chest. "Because I'm the one with the crush on you. You can't get one on me!"

Luke paused. "I thought you said you didn't have one for me anymore." He said it carefully, as if he wanted me to understand each syllable.

"Well, I lied."

"Well, good." His voice rose to match mine. "We like each other. So let's go steady."

"No," I said, my body instantly tightening.

Luke wanted to be my boyfriend. I couldn't believe it. He actually wanted to be with me. I frowned. Had I just told him no?

In the gleam of his Mustang headlights, I watched his teeth clench. "Hey, you started this," he accused. "I was ready to leave you alone, but you called me. You asked me out here."

I glanced away. "I just wanted a Fourth of July poem," I said. I wanted to remind him I wasn't good enough for him, so he should quit teasing me like this.

"You're still lying, aren't you?" he said.

When I spun to glare at him, he shook his head sadly. "I don't know what you're scared of, Carrie. Maybe it's the same thing I am. This isn't easy for me, either. I've never—" He broke off suddenly to run his hands through his hair.

I didn't pressure him to go on because he was right. I was scared. I was petrified of letting him get too close. I wound my arms around myself and rocked a little, realizing I was a fool.

Luke said, "You'll change your mind." And then as if someone turned on a light from night to day, his demeanor changed. Suddenly very abrupt and distant, he stood up and wiped his pants. "It's getting cold."

My arms only tightened their hold. "It was always cold."

"I should get you home. What time is it?"

"I don't know. Does it matter?"

"No. You're right. It doesn't matter. Let's get in the car." He reached down to help me to my feet. I hadn't realized how much I'd drunk until I stood and it all rushed to my head. I swayed a little and Luke caught me to him. "Time to get the drunkard home," he said, and pitched the rest of the bottle toward the ditch.

"You're littering," I told him. And when he started to lead me to the car, I said, "And I'm not drunk. I'm just dizzy. Stood up too fast."

He insisted I was definitely buzzed. But I didn't care. I was in love. I was in love with Luke Carter. I wasn't wasted enough to blab that out to him but I was pleasantly buzzed to the point where everything felt intense. As did the pain. I couldn't believe myself. Here he was, spilling his heart out at my feet, and I said no. Not only did I say no, I refused to take it back and tell him I really didn't mean no.

Luke patiently helped me into the passenger's seat but when he tried to put my seatbelt on, I swatted his fingers away and told him I could do that myself. He raised his hands in surrender and backed off to let me finish belting myself in.

The ride home took forever. I think he drove slowly on purpose. It wasn't because he was buzzed too. He'd only taken that one sip. So maybe it was because he wanted to stretch his time with me.

I was purposely quiet. If I spoke, I thought I might say something I would regret—something like, "Yes, I'll go out with you." I had this image in my head of doing exactly that, of flinging my arms around him and saying, "Yes, darling, I'm yours." And that's when he'd push me away and start laughing. "Gotcha!" he'd say. And it would be spread around as a big joke that Luke Carter had made a complete fool of Carrie Paxton.

That had to be the case because there was no way Luke could like me just because I was me. It went against all the rules of social order in Stillburrow.

I must've dozed off thinking through the whole

scenario because when Luke pulled up to the curb by my house, I was already half asleep. I yawned.

"Do you want me to walk you up?" he asked.

I opened my eyes and looked toward my home. My front walkway loomed before me. The house had never seemed so far from the curb as it did then. "No. I'll be fine."

"What're you going to tell your parents if they smell the wine on you?"

"I'll tell them you spilled it on me," I said, cracking a smile.

"Oh, that's great. Let your mom and dad think I'm some kind of alcoholic. They'd never let me see you again."

I stared at the dark windows of my house. I repeated the words *never let me see you again* over and over through my head. But they just didn't sound real.

"I don't think I have to worry about it," I said. "Looks like they're already asleep, anyway."

Luke shook his head, though. "They just want you to think that. My mom always catches me sneaking in too late by hiding out in the dark."

I glanced over at him and cocked an eyebrow. "Do you sneak in late a lot, Mr. Carter?"

He cleared his throat and refused to incriminate himself. "Let me walk you up," he said.

I flung open my door. "I can walk perfectly fine, thank you." I slurred the words a little as I set one foot outside, intending to show him just how capable I was. But he caught my arm.

"Wait." I glanced back to see him lean toward me. "Aren't you going to say goodbye?"

"Bye," I answered.

His lips curved. His hand moved down until it captured my fingers. He tugged me closer to him.

"Good night, Carrie Paxton," he said, barely moving. "Have sweet dreams about me."

"Actually, I'm thinking about dreaming of roller coasters. It feels like I'm on one."

Luke laughed and kissed me. It wasn't like our first kiss. This one was rougher. He yanked me to him and mashed his mouth to mine. And he didn't wait long before he let his tongue plunder. His fingers tightened their grip.

As dizzy as I already was, he threw me completely off balance. I reached up and cupped his cheek to steady myself. The stubble under my fingers shocked and delighted me. This was a man. I was kissing a man. I felt so grown up and mature.

This kiss was hotter and longer than the first one, and Luke pulled away before I did. When he did, he had a smug smile on his face. He rested his forehead against mine.

I closed my eyes and his fingers found my hair. "Come eat at my house tomorrow," he said. His voice was quiet and coaxing and I almost said yes. And then I realized...

"But tomorrow's Thanksgiving." I opened my eyes and pulled back to look at him.

"I know."

"I always have a big get-together with my family at Aunt Kay's house."

"Then stop by and see me afterward. It's just across the street."

I shook my head. The truth was I was scared to death of meeting his parents. I knew who Mr. and Mrs. Carter were. But I'd never talked to them face to face. I remembered when I was little and I'd sit outside the bank president's office next to Mom while I watched my father go inside and shake Mr. Carter's hand. But that was about as close as I'd ever gotten to the man. I think Luke knew about my fear of his parents but he didn't bring it up. And I was glad he didn't force the issue.

Instead, he sighed. "Fine." He let each lock of my

hair slip one by one from his fingers. "I'll let you go for now, then." He sounded wistful, like he already missed me. I thought it was possible only because I already missed him. "Goodnight, Carrie."

"Goodnight," I slurred back, right before I slipped out of the car and stumbled my way up the front walk. Luke didn't drive off until he saw me open the door. I moved inside, smelling of wine and burnt sulfur from the fireworks. The house was dark and silent. My over-trusting parents were asleep in their beds and I was a changed person. I'd just given a part of my soul away to Luke Carter, whether he knew or wanted it, or not.

****

When Thanksgiving Day came, I missed him. I was tempted to show up at his house, but I still had that fear of meeting his parents and that they'd instantly realize I wasn't good enough to date their son.

So I went with my mom and dad to the house across the street. Jordan was there, and she talked and talked to me about all the different boyfriends she had back at her school in Paulbrook. I was startled to learn she was doing things I'd just now experienced with Luke. I wanted to say, "But you're only twelve." I'm sure though, if I'd told my story to someone older, they'd have said, "But you're only sixteen." And that was the last thing I wanted to hear. So I kept quiet and only listened to Jordan's tales.

Marty actually showed up but he was late. We'd already cut into the turkey and Aunt Kay had said the prayer. I knew instantly something was wrong with him when he stumbled in. The first thing I did was sniff his shirt to see if he'd been drinking but he passed that test. All I could smell on him was the grocery store.

He glared at me when I leaned in and I quietly

said, "What's wrong with you?"

"I've got to spend the afternoon with you," he said. But he didn't have that mischievous grin he usually did when he said such things.

His clothes were rumpled like he'd slept in them. Yeah, I know, I know. He wasn't living at home anymore so there was no reason his clothes should be starched and ironed. He looked terrible, though. Maybe if he'd had his shirt tucked in and his hair combed, I might not have noticed. But the flicker in his eyes was...well, I couldn't explain it. I'd never seen Marty look this way before. He seemed drained and exhausted yet edgy and on alert. It was like he'd just beaten off an attacker but was braced for another assault.

"Are you on drugs?" I hissed in his ear.

He put his hand on my forehead and pushed me away. I took that as a no.

I'm not sure if anyone else noticed. They were so tickled to have him in their company again, they overlooked any problems. Mom stayed by his side throughout the meal and told him everything that'd been happening in the house since he'd been gone. Dad didn't say much. But his, "It's good to see you, son," revealed his pleasure.

The entire lunch felt phony. Everyone except Marty and me plastered on fake smiles and passed pasta around, making jokes about how the turkey would turn out this year.

Mom asked if she could refill Marty's glass with iced tea. When he lowered his head and said he was fine, she poured anyway and kept talking to him like he was interested. When she got into gossiping about Luke spending two evenings at our house, Marty's head shot up and he nailed me with an intense look. I wasn't sure what the warning in his gaze meant, but I met it and stared back at him, lifting an eyebrow and daring him to say something about *my* love life. Finally, he glanced away. Mom had already started in about our neighbors across the street getting their driveway paved.

When we went home, Marty came with us. For some reason, he'd walked to Aunt Kay's for Thanksgiving dinner. I don't know, maybe he just needed a good walk to clear his head. All I knew was he came home with us.

Jordan, Uncle Stan, and Aunt Kay waved us off and Marty sat in the back seat next to me for the short ride. It surprised me at first that he'd said OK to Mom's invitation to supper. He rested his head against the window and stared out as Mom chattered away in the front seat. I was sure something bad was going on with him then.

Marty waited half an hour after we made it home before he dropped the bomb. Since I already knew something was up, I'd been hanging around the living room to get in on the action when things went down. Marty was sitting in the middle of the sofa, not leaning back but with his back straight like some kind of guest. Mom had situated herself next to him. Dad was relaxing in his recliner with the footrest kicked up, and I lay sprawled on the loveseat, letting my feet dangle over the armrest.

"Mom, Dad," Marty said, taking in a deep breath, "I need to tell you something."

I stopped swinging my foot, knowing this was it. Mom took his hand and smiled. "What is it, honey?"

He licked dry lips and stared down at the floor. He nodded his head a little as if giving himself a mental pep talk before speaking. Then he said, "Abby's pregnant."

My feet hit the carpet floor and I sat up just as Mom covered a gasp with her hands. "Oh! Oh no," she moaned.

"Who's Abby?" Dad said.

Mom's eyes flashed to his. "Dean," she hissed. "I

told you Martin was seeing Abby Eggrow."

Dad scratched his chin then, as if his beard was itching. Slowly, he lowered the footrest of his chair. When he was in the upright position, he calmly folded his hands in his lap and eyed Marty critically. "Eggrow?" At Marty's nod, he continued. "She any relation to the principal?"

"She's his daughter," Marty said quietly.

Dad nodded thoughtfully, as if letting that soak in. "Does he know?"

"She said she was going to tell her family today."

Mom started to weep into her hands. She looked frail as she leaned away from Marty. I sank further into the loveseat, hoping it would swallow me whole, and suddenly, I couldn't breathe. It felt as if an anvil had been laid on my chest.

My brother had gotten a girl pregnant.

Dad stood and patted Mom on the back.

But she pushed his hand away. "Don't touch me."

"Now, Andrea." He sat next to her. "Just calm down. It's not that bad. Think about it on the bright side. We're going to be grandparents."

"No," she cried out and jumped to her feet. I think she startled everyone in the room because we all gawked at her. She glared at Marty. "How could you do this? How could you do this to such a nice girl like Abby Eggrow? How could you do this to me?"

Marty said nothing. What *could* he say? He lowered his head.

Mom wiped at the tears that were flooding her cheeks. "Do you not think at all, Martin? What were you thinking?"

"I wasn't," he said.

Dad had to turn his back to them as Mom laid into Marty. I cradled my stomach and tried not to cry.

When the front doorbell rang, I jumped. Mom

immediately wiped her eyes and turned away. Marty buried his face in his hands. My head swerved around to gawk at the door. Only Dad had the presence of mind to stride to the entrance and answer the bell. I was certain it would be some Eggrow, either Mr. or Mrs., here to beat Marty to a pulp, or maybe it was Abby herself, running to Marty for support. I had no thought the caller would be for me. So when Luke filled the open doorway, I jumped to my feet and let out a gasp.

My heart sank as my father's voice echoed back to me. "Not tonight, Luke. Carrie can't see you right now."

Luke glanced past him, right at me, saw my pale face and then looked over to Marty and Mom. He took a step back and nodded to Dad. Then he sent one last look my way before Dad shut the door in his face. When my father turned back to the family, his eyes slid accusingly toward me. I noticed then that Mom and Marty were also glaring at me like I was the guilty party here. I clenched my jaw and said nothing.

The silence was oppressive. I slid back down onto the loveseat. Finally, Dad turned to Marty. "Well, what're you going to do about all of this?"

Mom huffed out an angry sound and started in again, but Dad finally had control. "Andrea," he said in warning. "That's enough. What's done is done. We've got to see about fixing it as best we can now."

Mom glared at him, then spun away and left the room. Marty jumped when she slammed her bedroom door. He scrubbed the back of his neck with his hand.

"I don't know what to do, Dad," he said, so quietly I was afraid I'd misheard him at first.

But Dad came and sat next to him. "I wish I could tell you. I wish I could fix this for you, but you're a man now, Martin. And you've got to make a decision your mom and I can't make for you." Dad blew out a breath. "There comes a time in a person's life when they have to make a choice and there is no easy solution—when either option means a big change."

Marty glanced up at him and nodded. "I guess you're right. I've got to do this by myself." He ran the back of his hand across his nose and sniffed. Then he set his palms on his knees and rose to his feet. "I think I need to talk to Abby and get everything straightened out."

Dad laid a supporting hand on Marty's back. "I'll tell you one thing. You're a Paxton. You're my son. And I'm confident you'll do the right thing. I'll support you any way I can."

"Thanks, Dad," Marty told him and held out his hand. "I'm glad you didn't lose it like Mom did. I really needed to hear a reasonable voice right now."

Dad nodded and walked him to the door. He handed Marty his coat. "Don't worry about your mother. After the shock wears off, she'll be better." When Marty only lowered his head, Dad patted him on the back and opened the door. "She'll come around. Before you know it, she'll be buying baby toys by the carload."

Marty lifted his face and gave Dad a half smile that said he wanted to believe him but couldn't. My brother glanced briefly at me and then left.

Dad shut the door behind him, but didn't lower his hand. He stared at his fingers on the doorknob for a while. Then he dropped them and sighed. When he turned, he saw me still hovering on the loveseat. He paused.

It was only five in the evening, but he said, "Go to bed, Carrie."

Chapter Twelve

Mom discovered her wine bottle was missing the morning after Thanksgiving. I was still asleep.

Though Dad had told me to go to bed the night before when it was still light out, I hadn't actually fallen asleep until well after midnight. I'd gone to my room and only once did I try to sneak out to call Luke. I needed to explain to him what he'd seen earlier plus I had to tell someone the news.

I knew Luke would keep his mouth shut about it, especially if I blackmailed him with his own little poetry-writing secret if I thought he might blab. But when I tiptoed out of my room I ran into Dad in the hallway. He was staring at his closed bedroom door. I could hear Mom moving around inside. In my father's eyes, I saw anguish and the aching desire to go into that room with her.

His gaze shot to mine when he saw me approach.

I stopped short.

"What do you need?" he said in a sharp manner.

"I, uh…" I glanced hopefully around for a sign of the phone. "I was just getting a drink."

He nodded once and I dashed into the kitchen, filled a glass with tap water, and quickly retreated to the harbor of my messy lair. I sat on my mattress and sipped the water. It was incredibly warm, so I spit it back into the cup and set it on my nightstand.

Marty was going to be a daddy. I was going to be an aunt. There was going to be a baby. I tried to imagine Abby as a part of the family. I set up a picture in my head of her and Marty coming through the door for a Christmas celebration, a wide grin on his face as he carried a heaping pile of wrapped gifts. Abby tagged regretfully along behind him, toting a blond-headed child on her hip. She didn't smile as she set the toddler on the floor as soon as she stepped inside. The little boy wobbled across the ivory carpet with his arms spread open, ready to be held by the first person to reach him.

Then I pictured myself sitting across from her at our family table. She made this disgusted face as Dad started talking about motor problems. The little tow-headed boy in the high chair next to her picked up his plate and smashed it upside down on the table. Mom scurried to her feet for a washrag and Abby yelled at him.

I shivered and shook my head. It didn't seem possible. A baby? No, it was too weird to be true.

I tossed and turned half the night, thinking about how my mother and father had responded to the news, worried how Marty was holding up, and wondering how Principal and Mrs. Eggrow had reacted when they learned. And I thought of Luke.

He'd come to see me on Thanksgiving Day. It put a warm spot in my heart. I was sure I'd figure out a way to see him the next day but it turned out Mom had different plans.

She woke me by slamming open my door and ripping the covers off me. I winced and curled into a ball.

"Mom," I groaned, groping for my blankets. I opened one eye to discover them at the foot of the bed.

"Get up, Carrie." Mom's voice brooked no room for discussion. "We need to talk."

My eyes opened fully then. It felt early but it was late enough for the room to be flooded in light. I blinked a couple of times and finally sat up. I shivered, then reached for the blankets and pulled them over my legs. "What?" I said, and yawned.

Mom loomed over me with a drill sergeant's stance, her jaw set and her hands fisted in a pair of yellow dishwashing gloves. She brought the very potent aroma of lemon-scented disinfectant with her.

I forgot to mention earlier how she deep-cleaned when she was upset. She didn't just dust and vacuum; she got down on her elbows and scrubbed when something was troubling her. And from the smell permeating my room, I figured she must've been at it for a while.

She thumped one foot repeatedly against the floor and folded her arms. "There's a wine bottle missing from the kitchen drawer."

I stopped in the middle of a full body stretch. My arms fell limply down to my side.

I was busted. But I didn't go down lightly.

With all the innocence I could muster, I said, "There is?"

"Don't play dumb with me." She was loud enough for anyone inside the house to hear. "I didn't take it. And I've already asked your father. He didn't take it. Your brother doesn't live here anymore. So that just leaves you."

I attempted to move deeper inside the warmth of my blanket. "Are you sure there's one missing?" I tried.

"Carrie," she said, her voice stern.

"OK," I said, dropping my eyes. "I took it." My words were mumbled, but she heard me just fine.

"Where is it?"

I shrugged. In some ditch, busted by the side of the road. "It's gone."

"You drank the entire bottle by yourself?" At my lack of answer, she hissed out a long breath. I glanced up and shrank even further away. If she'd looked upset before, she was completely ticked off now. "You shared it with that boy, didn't you?" She spat out "that boy" like it was some kind of despicable disease.

I wanted to ask since when had Luke turned into "that boy"? This was the same guy she'd practically pushed me into being alone with in my bedroom. But I already knew the answer. It was since my brother had come home with the news he'd impregnated Abby Eggrow.

"That's it," she said, her voice rough and angry. "You're grounded."

My jaw fell loose. "Grounded?" I'd never been grounded in my entire life. I wasn't even sure what the punishment entailed.

"You stole from your parents," Mom said, lifting her index finger. "You lied to us." She lifted a second finger. "And you drank under age." Up with finger number three. "So you've broken the state law along with the laws of this house." She turned away disgusted. "And I don't know how many other things you've done.

"I expect you to be more responsible than this, Carrie. Alcohol is a dangerous thing. At first, you think you've having fun and then the next thing you know, you're pregnant and getting married at age eighteen." She pinned me with a sudden glare. "How many times have you snuck out of the house to be with him?"

I shook my head. "Mom, it's not what you think. We're not—"

But she held up an I-don't-care hand and said. "How many times?"

My shoulders fell and my head dropped. I stared at the hands I had folded in my lap. "Just that once," I said. Then I remembered the first ride he'd given me in his Mustang. Our first kiss. "Twice," I quickly amended.

Mom sighed in disgust. Then she tossed a dusting rag and a can of furniture polish onto the mattress beside me. "Clean this mess," she ordered. "And when you're done in here, wipe out the shelves in the kitchen."

She stormed out, leaving the door wide open. I was left in my room, barely awake and still in my pajamas. This wasn't how I'd expected to start my day. I crawled out of bed, not bothering to make it, and started picking things up from the floor.

This was grossly unfair. Marty had knocked up some girl and I was the one who ended up grounded? OK, so it'd been wrong to swipe the wine. But come on. I'd never done anything even remotely bad before. Didn't I deserve some kind of reprieve for a first-time offense?

I guess not, because Mom frequently came to the doorway to check my progress. Sometimes, she'd throw out orders, telling me to make my bed or fold that pile of clothes or stack that pile of books straighter. It was just before noon when Luke called.

I'd finished my room and had all the plates and cups piled on the kitchen table while I stood on the countertop and wiped out each empty shelf. Mom sat at the table, apparently reading a book, though she never turned a page, just gazed sightlessly at the words and said nothing. When the phone rang, I immediately shimmied off the countertop. "I'll get it."

"You will not," Mother said, and slammed the book closed. She sent me a glare that had me climbing back on the counter, wiping away.

In the front room, I heard her say, "Hello, Luke...No, she can't come to the phone right now. Carrie's grounded...No...Thank you for calling. Have a nice weekend." She hurried the last part, like she was interrupting something he'd been saying, and then she hung up. When I saw her appear out of the corner of my eye, staring me down, I acted like I was pouring all my attention into scrubbing the top shelf.

"Do we need to get a pregnancy test taken for you too?" she finally asked.

After pausing a moment to discover I wasn't actually going to sink through the floor from mortification, I lifted my chin high and said, "No, we most certainly do not."

She sniffed at my bitter tone like she didn't believe me, but after that she turned away, left me alone in the kitchen, and never broached the subject again.

I spent the rest of Thanksgiving break cleaning. Through the remainder of Friday and all day Saturday, neither Mom nor I left the house. She kept busy by finding things for me to do. I polished windows, washed curtains, scrubbed the walls and dusted every inch of wood to a reflecting shine.

Mom told Dad about the wine at lunch on Friday. He said nothing but looked at me with distinct disappointment, which made me lower my head in guilt. That man could pack more blame in one look than Mom could in two days' worth of cleaning duty.

On Sunday, she couldn't find anything else for me to clean. I sat between her and Dad through church. Marty didn't show but neither did any of the Eggrows. After lunch, I was sent to my room where I remained the rest of the day. We didn't hear from Marty. Mom and Dad didn't call him either, to see if he was all right. And I couldn't be freed to go search him out. So none of us knew how the Marty-Abby situation was progressing.

It was Monday morning before I got wind of any late-breaking news. I arrived late to school, running in the front door after the first bell had already rung. Mom and Dad had argued the night before in their bedroom. I could barely hear them through the wall, so it was hard to make out specific words, but the tone of voice was clear.

I lay in the dark, waiting for the discussion to come to a close, but it dragged on. I heard Marty's name mentioned a few times. Sometimes, Dad would say, "He's got to live his own life, Andrea." Finally Mom said, louder than before, "He should've learned something from our mistake."

Everything grew incredibly quiet after that. My eyes stung and I strained to hear my father say, "I didn't realize you thought of our life together as a mistake."

Not much was said after that and their words grew increasingly quiet. Finally, I heard the door open. It clicked so softly I hardly caught the sound. But then muffled footsteps moved down the hall past my door and into the living room. They didn't return while I was awake. I wondered which one of them had stayed on the couch.

The next morning, I slept in. My eyes hurt when I woke. Dried tears were crusted to my cheeks. Dad was already out in the shop when I dared to leave my room and Mom was in the kitchen with her legs crossed under the table, sipping coffee and staring at an old family picture on the wall.

I ate a silent and speedy breakfast with her but spent too long in the shower. I dawdled over getting dressed and didn't leave the house until Mom called to me, telling me it was getting late. I couldn't find all the homework and books I needed for school. It was hard to locate my stuff since Mom had made me clean my room.

Students were already clearing the halls and teachers were pulling their classroom doors shut when I raced through the front doors. It was a shock to see Luke standing next to my locker, pacing. His hands were in his pockets and he looked like an expectant father outside the door of a delivery room.

He took a step in my direction when he caught sight of me.

"What's going on?" he said instantly. He crowded in around me as I dropped my book bag by my locker and began working on the combination of my lock.

"I'm late," I said. My voice was breathless and harried. I opened the locker door and it covered his face. He made a sound of disgust and moved it so it opened the entire way and he could lean toward me as I dug inside my cubby.

"Your mom said you were grounded."

"Oh, yeah." I made it sound like I'd forgotten all about that torture, and I yanked out the supplies I needed for first hour. I glanced up at Luke and saw the concern on his face. Then I wiped my bangs out of my eyes and said, "She found out about the wine."

Luke glanced up and down the empty halls and leaned closer. "No wonder she sounded so ticked off on the phone."

I blew out a breath and slammed my locker. "Let's just say it was a bad weekend all around."

"Why?" Luke followed close behind me as I started up the hall toward my classroom. "Something else happened, didn't it?" His fingers wrapped around my upper arm, pulling me around to face him.

"You're going to be late for class too," I said.

"What's going on, Carrie?" he said in a low demand.

I sighed and checked the quiet halls. "I'll talk to you later, OK?"

He nodded, bobbing his head quickly, while giving me a concerned look. His fingers squeezed briefly, and then he let go, racing down the hall in the opposite direction toward his own class. The bell rang just as I eased inside the room. The teacher slid me a short, condemning look and then waited to start until I slumped into the first available seat.

I noticed it immediately: the stares and the whispers.

I saw more than one person glance at me and then away when I caught them doing so. The teacher also noticed the lack of attention and spent a couple of minutes lecturing us about talking while she was trying to teach. But as soon as she started teaching again, someone would turn around and whisper something to the person behind them.

Finally, the teacher gave up and assigned us extra homework. Whispers continued to circulate around me and glances steadily hit in my direction. I figured it was about Abby and Marty. Pregnancy was big news in our school since girls so rarely came up pregnant before they left the twelfth grade.

There'd probably only been a dozen or so high school girls who'd gotten pregnant since my mom had had her turn years ago. Now it was the son she'd been carrying who'd caused the damage.

When the bell rang, students swarmed into the halls spreading gossip like a brush fire. I followed at the end, feeling like the spark that had lit the fuse. People stopped talking and stared at me when I passed. "That's her," I could almost hear them snicker behind their hands. "Marty Paxton's sister." I began to feel like I was the one who was pregnant.

I caught E.T. near my locker. He seemed leery about approaching me, but I grabbed his arm and dragged him with me as I went by.

"What's going on?" I hissed, even though I was already sure I knew.

"Is Abby Eggrow really pregnant?" was all he could say.

"Where'd you hear that?"

He shrugged. "I don't know. *Everyone's* been asking me since I'm your friend and you're Marty's sister, and he's roommates with my brother." He puffed out his chest a little, like that gave him importance. "Is it really Marty's kid?"

"Look," I said, and edged in closer to him so I could speak confidentially, "that's nobody's business but Abby and Marty's. Who started the rumor, anyway? Does Egghead know about it?"

E.T.'s eyes shot open wide and his head bobbed. "He knows," he said in a horrified whisper. "I saw him storming down the halls right after class. He's fuming."

"Well I would be too if everyone was spreading rumors like that about my daughter."

"Rumors?" E.T. frowned at me. "She's not pregnant, then?"

I sighed. "I guess you'll find out in nine months when she does or doesn't have a baby, won't you?"

E.T. gave me a disappointed look. "Fine," he said, already turning away. "Don't tell me."

"Fine, I won't," I called after him. "And quit spreading gossip. It's beneath you, E.T."

I had to go the bathroom before the next class started, making me almost late again. The girls in there shut up when they saw me enter and they quickly began to file out. I turned on the water and let it spray out into my cupped hands. I dipped my head and wet my face, shuddering when the icy cold droplets hit my nose and cheeks. When I dabbed myself dry with a handful of paper towels, I stared at my reflection in the mirror.

This was not the way I'd wanted to end my terrible weekend. But I should've expected it. Of course the news would leak and spread. I knew that. I just hadn't been aware it would seep out so fast or that it'd personally affect me.

Liz and Jill came inside the bathroom but pulled up short when they caught sight of me. Then they glared and folded their arms until I dropped my head and murmured an, "Excuse me." I brushed past them and fled. I wasn't sure if they held me responsible for Marty and Abby's actions or what, but I could tell I wasn't on their A-list.

I could've stuck around and defended myself but I didn't feel like going into a battle at the moment. If they wanted to be mad at me for something my brother and their friend had done, then I wasn't going to cry about it and throw a fit. They could think whatever they wanted. I didn't care about their opinions.

Suddenly, I wanted to see Luke, but I missed him in the halls.

My next class was history with Mr. Decker. It was the class I shared with Abby, but she wasn't present when I arrived and she never showed. When the sign-up sheet hit my desk, I read the word *Excused* by her name. I'd just signed my own name on the list when the secretary's voice came through the intercom.

"Mr. Decker?"

The teacher paused and looked toward the speaker box at the corner where the ceiling met the wall. "Yes?"

"Could you send Carrie Paxton to the principal's office, please?"

Mr. Decker glanced at me. "Sure," he called.

Chapter Thirteen

The principal of SEC shut the door to his office. I was already seated at the chair in front of his desk when he came in, but I had no idea what this was about. I figured it had to involve Marty, but why would Abby's dad want to talk to me about that? I would've thought he'd prefer to avoid me.

Mr. Eggrow came around his desk silently and sat in his chair. He rested his elbows gingerly on his desktop and stared at me as he folded his hands, carefully interlacing each finger. I sank back in the chair. For a moment, he said nothing and my eyes began to wander around the room, catching sight of pictures on the wall of Abby and her sister, Sidney.

Finally, he spoke. "Do you know what the penalty is for defamation?"

I frowned. "Defamation?" I said slowly.

His voice rose to a harsh, almost uncontrolled pitch. "Lying about another individual, Miss Paxton." He spat out the name Paxton like it was a piece of stale gum he needed to be rid of.

My mouth worked. "I don't..." What in God's name was he talking about? "No, I don't know the penalty."

"People go to jail for it," he said. He was quickly losing control of the anger I could see simmering just beneath the surface, and I was becoming increasingly confused. But *defamation*? I tried to think of anything I might've written in the paper but came up blank.

"Not only does it hurt the person being lied about, but it decreases the worth of the person spreading the lie as well. I hope you realize the destruction you've not only done to this school, but what you're doing to yourself."

My chest sucked in around my ribs when I inhaled sharply. I shook my head. "I'm sorry, but I have no idea what you're talking about."

He stood up slowly, his fingers flexing into a fist and then loosening. My eyes bugged. I had the feeling he wanted those constricting fingers wrapped around my neck. It didn't matter that his wide desk was between us. His looming stance scared the living daylights out of me. "Lies have been going around this school that my daughter's pregnant, and I know you started them."

I shot to my feet. *"What?!"*

"I'm giving you out-of-school suspension and refusing you any make-up homework. Your mother's already been called, so you can leave right now." My mouth dropped open as he nailed me with a menacing glare. "I don't want to see you in these halls for the rest of the week."

"But I didn't—"

He held up his hand and looked away. His jaw worked a few times before he hissed, "Just leave, Carrie."

My chin trembled. "Mr. Eggrow, I swear I didn't say anything about Abby to anyone. And besides, it couldn't be defamation because it's not a lie. She is pregnant. Marty told us—"

I knew the instant I said it, I shouldn't have. His eyes flashed warningly and his hand fisted again. But this was injustice. I had to defend myself.

"I'm aware your brother went to your house and told your family that," he said with strained patience. "But we've taken Abby to a real doctor since and had everything checked. She is definitely not pregnant."

The air left my lungs. Not pregnant? All this fuss and the girl wasn't even pregnant? I shook my head and stared at the desktop. Why hadn't Marty called and straightened everything out? My parents were fighting, my schoolmates were gossiping, and all because someone wasn't pregnant?

"Pregnant or not pregnant," I said, using the calmest voice I had, "I didn't talk to anyone. Mr. Eggrow, I don't—"

"Get out of here!" He roared it so loudly I jumped. "Get out of my office. Get out of my school." He started around his desk after me. "Get out of my town."

I stifled a scream and fled. The doorknob seemed slippery under my palm and I could almost feel how his hand would clamp around the back of my throat and squeeze if he caught me. But then I pulled hard and yanked the door open, flying into the secretary's domain. Egghead slammed the door shut behind me. Again, my body jerked. My hand came up to muffle a sob. Two secretaries sat at their desks watching me. One gave me a sympathetic look while the other glared.

I swept by them and dashed out into the hallway. I sprinted all the way to my locker, not caring that I wasn't supposed to run in the halls. Egghead could give me another week's worth of suspensions for all it mattered. As I raced by opened doors of classrooms, I caught glimpses of students seated at their desks. I didn't care if they gawked after me either. I just had to get out of there.

I reached my locker in record time and tore off the lock, throwing open my door. I'm not sure what I was thinking. I just started pulling things out, stuffing them into my bag. At that moment, I believed I'd never return to this blasted place. I would drop out before I stepped one foot inside

Egghead's school. There was another small town between Stillburrow and Paulbrook. It had a high school as well. I could enroll there, borrow one of Dad's cars off the lot and drive to school every morning.

I didn't realize I'd started to hyperventilate until I heard an alarmed voice call my name.

"Carrie? Carrie!"

I was grabbed by the shoulders from behind and spun around. Luke's worried gaze was all I saw. It was hard to distinguish anything else about him, because he looked blurred through all the tears.

"What are you doing out here?" I managed to ask. My breathing shuddered as I tried to regain some oxygen.

"I saw you pass my class and asked if I could go to the bathroom." His fingers bit down. "What's going on?"

My shoulders collapsed and I hiccupped. My head fell forward and my entire body trembled. I dived against his chest and fisted my hands around the cloth on the back of his shirt.

"I thought he was going to kill me," I rasped. "I was so scared, I thought…"

I couldn't talk. I can say now—since it's all over—I was acting completely irrational. But at the moment, I was petrified. I started blubbering all over Luke, not bothering to check my uncontrolled behavior. He kept saying, "Who," and "What," but it didn't register.

He was warm and safe and his arms were wrapped around me, rocking me. That's all that mattered. I felt so secure in his embrace I almost passed out. My legs even started to give.

But then Luke shook me. "Stop it," he said. His voice was panicked. "Talk to me, Carrie."

I looked up at him through my tear-stained lashes. "Egghead just suspended me."

"What?" His mouth dropped and he took a step back.

The step not only put distance between the two of us but it seemed to put a little distance between the situation and me. My head cleared and I began to feel in control of my limbs again. I concentrated on settling my breathing.

Luke took a breath and ran a hand through his hair. "Why?"

I sniffed and wiped at my wet cheeks. "Because Abby's not pregnant."

"Huh?" He moved closer and lowered his head. "I think you need to tell me what happened this weekend."

I wiped back hair that had fallen in my face, trying to gain a little decorum. Luke lifted a hand to help. He tucked a strand behind my right ear. Our fingers brushed.

"I've been hearing the rumor all morning about her being pregnant," he said. "So it's not true, then?"

I shook my head. "I, ah..." I looked down, trying to ignore the queasy feeling in my stomach. "Marty told us she was pregnant on Thanksgiving Day. Right before you showed up, actually."

Luke nodded. "I could tell something big had just happened."

"But I guess she's not." I looked up to Luke and searched his eyes for a little faith. "I didn't tell anyone she was, though."

He snorted and gave a short laugh. "Of course you didn't. Why would I think..." His words died away as my meaning seemed to sink in.

"Her dad thinks I did," I said, and bit my lip. "I'm being suspended a week for defamation."

Luke's look said he didn't believe me. He laughed. "Yeah, right." But when I didn't join in, he stopped and stared at me dumbfounded. "But that's crazy."

"Get back to class, Luke."

We both jumped at the commanding voice that boomed from behind us. I spun around and so did Luke. The principal loomed in front of us with his arms held stiffly at his sides. My ears started to buzz and I shrank back, bumping into Luke. He took my arm and stepped in front of me, blocking me from the older man.

"Mr. Eggrow," he said, and his voice shocked me. It sounded so formal and rational. He was definitely the banker's son, his respectful courtesy layered over a thick air of authority. "I think there's been a misunderstanding. Carrie couldn't have started the gossip about—"

"Did you hear what I said?"

Luke backed down. At least I thought he had. "Yes, sir," he said. "But I'm telling you it's not possible that she could've started any gossip. I've been trying to get a hold of her all weekend. I wasn't even allowed to talk to her on the phone because she's been grounded. And she arrived to school late this morning. You see, there wasn't any time for her to spread—"

"Return to your class...now," Mr. Eggrow commanded.

But Luke's shoulders were stiff. "Do you have any proof the rumor was started by her?"

"Mr. Carter—" Mr. Eggrow's voice rose and echoed down the hall. I caught sight of a few teachers glancing out of their classrooms. And what a sight they must've seen...Luke Carter squaring off with the principal and Carrie Paxton hovering behind her brave defender.

"This is none of your concern. Now go back to class before I give you an after-school detention."

The breath rushed out of Luke. He glanced at me and then back to the principal. He licked his bottom lip. "I think I'll see her safely to the door first," he said, and took my arm. He turned us toward the first available exit and started dragging me down the hall.

"What are you doing," I said. "Are you crazy? Go to class." I glanced over my shoulder at Mr. Eggrow, whose silhouette was quickly becoming smaller and smaller.

"Shut up," Luke whispered back. "I wasn't about to leave you alone with him." At the door, he pulled me around to face him and tilted my chin up with his hand. "I'll take care of this. Don't worry about it." Then he pulled me onto the toes of my shoes for a quick yet hard kiss and pushed me out the door.

If I hadn't been so distraught about everything, I would've laughed. He'd acted like some knight in shining armor who'd just ridden up on his white stallion to rescue me and now was shooing me back into the castle (even though he'd actually sent me outside) while he set forth to save the day.

But at that moment, I couldn't think about it. I stopped at the top of the school steps and wondered what I was going to do next. I couldn't go home. I refused to go home. There was no telling what Mr. Eggrow had told Mom of my suspension. She probably thought I'd been caught in the halls doing the nasty with Luke. If I went home and told her why I'd really been suspended, she and Dad would get upset and charge toward the school. And that would really stir things. The real problem was with Marty and Abby. If my parents stormed the building and confronted Egghead, they'd only bring a personal problem onto school grounds where it most certainly didn't belong. Nope, I definitely couldn't go home.

Over on the east side of the building, I could hear the grade school kids playing at recess. I glanced over and watched three children chase each other. Suddenly I wanted to be that age again, where I didn't understand so much, where I didn't have to be responsible for anything, and no one could blame me for such huge catastrophes.

A teacher blew her whistle and the children made one last frantic circle around the jungle gym before they reluctantly ran toward her and lined up into sloppy, uneven rows. As they filed inside, I started down the steps. The first place I usually went to be alone was the park. But that was too close to home and my parents would probably find me there, and then I'd have to explain the whole suspension thing.

But the library was right across the street. I crossed the empty road and jogged up the wide marble steps of the library. A cold breeze flapped against the collar of my coat. I shifted my heavy book bag to my other shoulder and opened the door.

Silence seemed to waft out and greet me. I knew the librarian was usually at her desk, which was directly to the right. I didn't want her to see me and ask why I wasn't in school, so I entered quietly and turned straight to the left. I found a deserted corner, which wasn't hard since the tiny library was empty of patrons, and there I started my camp-out.

Since I wasn't going to be in school for a week, I thought I could come here in the days and study each class for an hour, the hour I should've been in that class. That way I wouldn't be so far behind next week.

I was no longer thinking about dropping out of SEC. I'd settled down a lot since that irrational moment in the hallway with Luke. I wasn't looking forward to going back after losing five days of class work, no, but I was thankful I wouldn't be missing any tests. And I was worried about the newspaper. I was the only member on the journalism staff who really did anything with *The Central Record*. The teacher was going to be pulling her hair out by

Friday when deadlines hit. I guess she'd just have to go to her friendly principal to complain if there were problems.

I tried to concentrate on reading through all the different textbooks, but it was near to impossible. Who actually read those books, anyway? Talk about dry writing. But I eventually came up with a way to amuse myself as I scanned. Here's an example of what I did. My history book quoted, "John Wilkes Booth, an unknown actor and southern sympathizer, assassinated President Abraham Lincoln at Ford's Theatre on April 14, 1865."

So I just penciled in my own translation in my notebook, writing, "It was April 14th and spring was blooming. Only days before, the North had won their grueling war. Life was good for the president and his wife. And what better way could they celebrate than to attend the distinguished Ford's Theatre and watch a relaxing play. But the South had one last attack before they would admit defeat. One man, John Wilkes Booth, who was a Rebel at heart, slipped into Abraham Lincoln's box seat and shot him in the back of the head, killing not only the man but the leader of this united nation."

OK, so it wasn't that exciting but writing helped me keep my mind off things. So I wrote and I wrote. Finally, it was late enough in the afternoon I felt I should start venturing from the library. I knew I should go home, to save myself from even more punishment for staying away. But there was another stop I needed to make first.

I seriously needed to see Marty. I walked along Birch Street and then up Adams. I passed Georgia's and ducked a quick peek through the windows to make sure my mom wasn't inside before I crossed the street toward the grocery store. When I pulled opened the door to Getty's General, the bell jingled over my head.

I skidded to a stop when I saw the owner of the store, and not my brother, at the cash register. There were only a handful of customers cruising the four aisles and no one was checking out at that moment. John Getty turned toward me. He had a ready smile on his face but it froze in place when he saw that it was a Paxton filling the entrance.

"Can I help you?" he said, through unmoving, stiff lips.

I shook my head and started to move in reverse. Where was Marty?

"I'm sorry," I said, right before I backed into the door. I groped behind me, pushed it open, and escaped.

What was going on? Why wasn't Marty at work? I started to breathe heavily, already suspecting the worst. I ran the whole way to his place. The small house he rented with Austin Fitz, owned by Austin's parents, was situated next door to the funeral home on Main Street. I pounded up their front steps and threw open the screen door. The regular door was already open and I charged in on Austin as he lay sprawled on the sofa in sweats, playing a video game on the television.

Austin, who looked nothing like his younger brother, E.T., worked nights at the gas station. He looked like he'd just awakened and gone straight to the television. His eyes were blurry and his hair was sticking up. An empty cereal bowl sat on the floor in front of him.

"Come on in," he called, even though I was already inside. He sent me a sleepy smile. "What's up, little sister?"

"Where's Marty?"

Austin's smile fell and he shook his head. "He ain't doing so well. The guy's bummed out, let me tell you."

"Where is he?" I repeated.

Austin shrugged. "Haven't seen him. I'd check his room if I were you."

I rolled my eyes and started toward Marty's room. I tried to open his door but it was locked. So I pounded.

"Marty! Open this door right now."

I continued to pound until the door cracked opened and my very mad-looking brother glared out at me. "Stop pounding," he said, wincing. "You're giving me a headache, stupid."

He looked about as bad as I'd ever seen him. Dark rings circled his sunken eyes and he hadn't shaved in a while. Strong whiffs of alcohol escaped from his room, choking me.

"Let me in," I said.

I tried to push my way inside, but the rest of his body was blocking the door. He snarled at me. "Cut it out. I'm not dressed"

I gave him a get-real look. "I'm not blind, Marty. I can see your shirt and jeans through the crack in the door." I put my weight against the wood. "I need to talk to you."

He didn't budge. "So talk."

I glanced toward the living room where his roommate was playing video games. Marty caught my meaning but only shrugged.

"Fine," I said. I crossed my arms over my chest and glared. "Egghead just suspended me for a week, thanks to you."

Marty glared at me for a moment. We had a small stare-off. We'd had hundreds of stare-offs over the years and we usually used them to determine if the other person was lying or not. I knew the routine so I gazed back, giving him my serious face.

When Marty was satisfied I spoke the truth, he squeezed his eyes shut and hissed out a curse. Then he stepped back and let me in.

Chapter Fourteen

"Why'd he suspend you?" Marty said, when he closed the door behind us

I felt like I'd been shut inside a dumpster. The stench of alcohol and other rotten things about knocked me over. It was chilly and damp and dark. Too cave-like for my comfort. Marty had even thrown blankets over the windows to keep out the light.

"Why aren't you at work?" I strode to the windows, tripping over shoes and pizza boxes and who knew what else on the floor as I went.

I yanked the sheets off, and daylight poured into the room.

Marty groaned and winced. "I liked them where they were," he said through clenched teeth.

I spun around to face him. He'd sat down on the edge of his unmade bed and was lifting his hand to shade his eyes.

"Did you get fired?"

Empty beer cans littered the floor between us. Dirty laundry was piled in various mounds around the room. Marty fell back on the mattress and stared up at the ceiling.

"Leave me alone," he said, closing his eyes.

I came to stare down at him. "Did they fire you?"

"Yes!" he yelled.

"Why?"

He spit out a contemptuous laugh. "Why do you think, brat? How much brainpower does it take to come up with that answer? Abby's mom is John Getty's little sister. And John was my boss. Why would he keep me around after all this?"

I sat down beside him. "Is she pregnant or not?"

Marty opened his eyes and they once again focused on the ceiling. His jaw moved and his Adam's apple slid up and then down as he swallowed.

"I guess not," he finally said.

I lay down then, next to him, and stared up at the ceiling as well. "So it's over between you two, huh?"

Marty gave another short laugh when he said, "Yeah."

"You're just going to stay in your room and get drunk, then?"

"It's the best plan I've thought up yet."

"I wouldn't take the sissy's way out if I were you," I said, propping my knees up and resting the soles of my shoes on his mattress.

Marty turned his head to glare at me. "Well, you're not me. Now get off my bed."

I didn't move except to let my knees sway back and forth. "What happened?"

Marty sighed. "Nothing. Why'd you get suspended?"

"Because Egghead thought I told everyone in school his daughter was pregnant." Because it'd been a few hours since that actual event occurred, I was able to speak of it clearly, almost as if I was proud of the fact.

Marty's eyes narrowed on me. "Did you?"

I slugged him in the arm. "No, you idiot. I did not. Why would I spread something like that? Even though I did think it was true until Egghead called me into his office and very distinctly clarified the facts of the situation."

Marty sat up so quickly he about had me rolling

off the side of the bed because of the sudden shift in weight on the mattress. He stared down at me, shocked. "He *told* you?"

I frowned. "Told me what?"

Marty instantly looked away. "Nothing."

I sat up then too. "What?"

Marty shook his head. "Never mind." He glanced at me. "Why didn't you just tell him you didn't start the rumors?"

My jaw dropped. "I did! The man wouldn't listen to a word I said. Let me tell you, he was mad!"

"So?" Marty set his feet on the floor and stared at the wall in front of him.

"So," I repeated. I frowned as I watched Marty hold his stomach and start to rock back and forth. Then I shook my head and tried to continue with my story. "So he was mad enough to charge at me."

"He what?" Marty looked at me sharply.

"He told me to get out of his office, but I was trying to explain my innocence." I shrugged. "I guess he got sick of it because he started around his desk like he was going to hurt me."

"That son of a..." Marty surged to his feet and started toward the door, swaying as he went.

I ran after him and grabbed his arm. I had to dig my feet into the floor to stop him. "Where do you think you're going?"

"I'm going to kill him."

"Marty!"

His hand was on the doorknob and he yanked it open. I kicked the door shut with my foot and jumped in front of it, blocking his path. My brother had murder in his eyes. I'd never seen him like this before. It scared me.

"Stop it," I said. "What's wrong with you?"

"What's wrong with me?" He pointed a finger at his chest and stared at me like he couldn't believe I didn't understand. "That man took away the only girl I ever cared about. He got me fired from my job. He killed my baby. And now he's threatening my sister. How much more do you expect me to take?"

I gasped. The news knocked the breath out of me. If I hadn't been leaning against the door, I would have had to grab it for support. Suddenly, I felt lightheaded. I guess Marty was dizzy too, because he wilted right there onto the floor in front of me and cradled his face in his hands.

I moved my hand over my stomach where my guts were twisting into knots. "What are you talking about, Marty?"

His speech was muffled in his hands as he moaned the words but I heard him clearly. "She was pregnant," he said. "I swear to God she was pregnant."

My knees gave out then. I knelt down in front of him and touched his shoulder. "You're not saying what I think you're saying, are you?"

He looked up at me and his eyes were rimmed in red. He sniffed. "I saw the two lines on the test. I...saw...them." He took my hands and squeezed. "There was a baby, Carrie. Two lines meant she was pregnant."

I shook my head.

But Marty nodded. "I went to her house right after I told Mom and Dad. She said her dad wanted to take her to a doctor in Paulbrook the next morning, to make sure it was true. But we'd already taken one of those home pregnancy things. We already knew she was pregnant."

He blew out a shaky breath. "I said OK, though, and I left her alone. I saw her and her dad leave the next morning when they drove by the house. It was nighttime before they got back." He swallowed and for a moment he couldn't talk.

I couldn't believe him. It just wasn't something that happened to someone from Stillburrow. I mean,

Mr. and Mrs. Eggrow dedicated their lives to children. Why would they...I shook my head. It wasn't possible.

Marty wiped at his eyes. "When I went to see her that night, she said there wasn't a baby after all and we should call things off." He rocked back and forth, staring at something on the wall. "About as soon as I got home, John called. He told me not to bother coming into work the next morning."

My brother winced as if he was going through the whole experience all over again. His shoulders shook and I did the only thing I could think to do. I hugged him. He buried his face in my shoulder and let loose. His sobs racked through both of us.

"I loved her," he said. "I really did. I thought we were going to get married and buy a house across from the park. I thought we were going to have a family. And I could start up my own business. Just like Dad."

And Abby would've been perfectly miserable, just like Mom. She'd pretend she had this perfect life and this happy little family, when all she wanted was something better.

"They didn't even ask me," he said.

I shook my head. "Maybe there never was a baby."

"There *was*."

"There wasn't," I snapped. "Marty look at me." I waited until he lifted his head. He puffed out a breath and then set his jaw. "It was all a mistake," I told him. "That first test was a dud. There was never a baby."

He wouldn't say it. He swallowed again and looked like he was about to burst. I grasped his hand. "Say it, please. It doesn't matter what really happened. If you're right, then it's already too late. There's nothing you can do about it. And if you're wrong, then you're lying about her, and Principal

Eggrow will accuse you of defamation too, except you won't get a suspension but jail time. So tell me there never was a baby. You have to believe this, OK?"

Marty rested his cheek against the wall and closed his eyes. "There was never a baby," he whispered. A tear trickled down his cheek and it was the last that fell. He opened his eyes and sat up, letting out a shaky breath. "I must've been mistaken."

That's when I wanted to cry. I got to my feet, unable to watch him. "Come on," I said, and briefly glanced down at him.

"Where?"

"Home," I said.

He shook his head.

And I nodded mine. "Mom will get a ton of food stuffed down you, and you can get some rest. You need to tell them there's no baby, anyway."

"I will," he said. "Just not yet. Can't go home yet. I'm not even sober."

I held my hand down to him, offering to help him to his feet. "Then come to the kitchen. It can't be healthy to stay in this room. Someone should put a caution sign on the door. Beware of Contamination. I'll fix you something to eat."

I smiled suddenly, thinking of Luke and the snack he'd shown me how to make. "I've got the perfect thing to feed you."

Finally, Marty let me help him to his feet. When we were both standing, he looked down at me. "Don't tell anyone what I said before. OK?"

I shook my head. "I won't."

Marty was quiet for a moment and then he said, "Let's get something to eat. What're you making?"

I grinned, trying to put some cheer into the mood. "It's really good," I said, opening his door. "Luke gave me the recipe."

Marty pulled up short and I glanced back. I did

a double take when I saw the horror on his face and stopped myself. "What is it?"

He grabbed my arm roughly and jerked me back inside the room. "You need to stay away from him, Carrie." I rolled my eyes and he yanked on my arm again. "I'm serious."

I shook free of his grip. "I can tell," I shot back and examined my arm for fingerprint marks.

"What do you think you're doing with that type of guy?"

I paused and carefully asked, "And what type is that?" But before he could answer, I went on, "Luke isn't the type you think he is. Besides, there's nothing going on between us." I shrugged. "Not technically, anyway."

"Not technically?" Marty shook his head. "What's that supposed to mean?"

"I don't know," I said, suddenly wondering myself what it meant. So far, we'd kissed twice. No, make that three times, since the kiss at school only hours ago. We'd discussed dating, yet only ended up fighting. We'd gone on two car rides alone into the country. And then there was that whole scene at school where he'd defended me to the principal.

Technically, I had no idea what that made us.

I glanced up at Marty. "Just don't worry about it, OK?"

That's when Marty shook me. "Haven't you learned anything from what just happened to me? I'm begging you, stay away from him, Carrie. Those type of people are bad news"

I had this impulsive urge to defend Luke. Marty was unjustly classifying him—just as I'd done. But now I knew Luke better and I was completely gone for him.

Still, I wasn't sure if there was anything there to stay away from. So I only nodded.

Marty hugged me briefly, tightly. "Thank you,"

he said. "I know you're not going to listen to me, but thanks for trying to make me feel better."

Then he pushed me away and said he was starving.

Austin followed us into the kitchen when he saw us pass, and it just so happened they had all the supplies for Luke's after-school special. I had to make a bowlful for each guy. Just as I was putting the supplies away, two more boys rushed inside the house. E.T. was followed by his twelve-year-old brother, Trevor.

"There you are," E.T. said, when he saw me. "We've been looking for you all over town." Winded, he plopped down in a chair next to Austin.

"Why?" I said, stuffing the ice cream back into the freezer.

E.T.'s eyes were bright. "Haven't you heard yet?"

"We even heard about it in the junior high," Trevor said, opening the freezer to take the ice cream back out. When he turned back, he blurted, "Did Luke Carter really kiss you right there in the hallway?"

E.T. shoved him toward the table and spun around to tell me *his* news. "Mr. Eggrow dropped your suspension."

"What?" I leaned against the counter, facing everyone. "Why? What happened?"

"Luke went around, asking everyone where they'd heard the rumor. And he found out who started it." E.T.'s eyes gleamed. He loved knowing something that no one else knew.

"Well, who was it?" Marty demanded.

E.T. slid my brother a nervous look and then said to me, "Sidney Eggrow."

"Sidney?" I blinked. Abby's own sister had started it? I didn't know what to say.

"Mr. Eggrow sent her home when he found out. She said she didn't mean for everyone to know. She only told one friend." E.T. shrugged. "But you know how that goes. She overheard Abby telling her parents that she thought she was pregnant. And no one knew Sidney heard it so they didn't know to tell her it wasn't true. But Mr. Eggrow called an assembly for the whole school in the auditorium and explained it was all a big misunderstanding. That Sidney heard something she wasn't supposed to hear and no one knew to tell her it wasn't true because they didn't know she knew."

E.T. shook his head. "It was really confusing. But then Luke stood up and asked right there in front of everyone if Mr. Eggrow was going to apologize to you for accusing you of defamation."

My hand flew to my mouth. "He didn't."

E.T. nodded and grinned. "He did. I called your house right after school. But your mom hadn't heard from you all day. She sounded real worried too because the school had already called twice to say you were suspended and then to say you could come back. She was pretty confused when I talked to her. By the way, she's looking for you right now too."

I glanced at the clock on the wall. "Oh no. It's already four."

"You better get home," Marty said.

I was halfway down Marty and Austin's front steps before I realized E.T. had followed me out.

"Hey," he said.

"What?" I turned back, impatiently staring up at him on the top step.

He opened his mouth and then shut it. Then he glanced down the street.

"Come on," I said. "You're making me even later."

He frowned down at me. "Are you going out with Luke Carter?"

It sounded odd to hear that spoken aloud by someone. Going out with Luke Carter? It just wasn't normal. But what was normal anymore?

I shrugged, and squinted up at E.T. "I don't know," I said.

"How can you not know?"

I tried to think up some way to explain it, but there really was no explanation unless I replayed the last few weeks and told him everything that had happened between Luke and me. And I didn't have time for that, so I just said, "It's complicated."

E.T. seemed to mull it over. Finally, he said, "I guess he's good enough for you."

Now that startled me.

I had no idea E.T. cared whether I dated anyone or not, or how they would treat me. He was the only friend I had at school. But we never really discussed personal things like feelings and that kind of junk. He was just the guy I always sat by and defended. It was touching to know he thought about me enough to worry about my life.

"You're not going to start ignoring me now that you've got a boyfriend, are you?"

I rolled my eyes. So much for the sweet E.T. who was only worried about me. "Shut up," I said.

He grinned and lifted one shoulder. "I didn't think you would."

I sighed. "Does that ease your worries? Can I go now?"

"Yeah," he said. "You can go now."

"Thank you, your highness." I bowed down to him and when I straightened, stuck my tongue out before racing across the street.

"Bye," he called after me. I glanced back and waved.

I ran the whole way home. It was four blocks and I was winded by the time I reached our yard. The sun was easing down below the horizon. I pulled up short when I spotted the white Mustang with black racing stripes parked out front.

Luke.

I dashed the rest of the way to the front door and flung it open.

He sat on the loveseat with his knees spread wide and his hands hanging down between them. His head was lowered but he raised it when the door opened. He stood when he saw it was me filling the entrance. Dad had been in his chair with the footrest down. He didn't bother to stand at my arrival. Luke took a step in my direction. But then Mom appeared in the kitchen doorway.

She rushed past him, crying out. "Where...have you...been?" She crushed me into a hug and then said. "Don't you ever do that to me again, young lady."

I pulled back. "I was at Marty's."

"The school called," she went on. "They started talking to me about your suspension and then they were saying it'd been dropped. I had no idea what was going on."

I lowered my head, kicked at a patch of carpet. "I was at the library studying until about two thirty. Then I went to see Marty." I looked up. "There's no baby."

"There's no baby?" she echoed.

I nodded. "Abby's not pregnant. It was all a misunderstanding." My voice choked a little then. I thought of the expression on Marty's face when he'd insisted there had been. "But Mr. Eggrow thought I'd told everyone there was, and he got mad."

Mom moved back a step. Her face was a little pale. "She's not pregnant?"

I shook my head. And my mother backed even further away. Dad pushed to his feet then. When she turned away from me and disappeared down the hall toward her room, Luke came to me.

He couldn't take his gaze off me. "Are you OK?" he said. His eyes moved from my face to my arms as if he were searching for physical wounds.

I nodded. "I'm fine."

His searching blue eyes returned to mine. "You weren't earlier."

I slipped a hand in my pocket and my eyes fell as I remembered exactly how I'd been earlier. "I'm better."

He said, "I guess you heard what happened," at the same moment I said, "E.T. told me what you did."

I lifted my face and we shared a moment where no words had to be spoken. The simple contact of our gazes was enough. Softly, I said, "Thank you."

He nodded once, and reached for my arm. But before he touched me, Dad's voice interrupted from behind us. Obviously, he'd been watching the whole scene.

"Carrie's still grounded."

Luke glanced over at him, a regretful—but almost defiant—look still on his face, like he wanted to argue with my father.

"Now that she's made it home safe and sound, you should be going, Luke."

It was clear from his expression that Luke didn't agree. "I need to tell her something," he finally said to Dad. "May I very quickly tell her something?"

Dad seemed to seethe at Luke for being brave enough to stand up to him. Finally, he said, "You can tell her as she walks you to the door." He turned on his heel and followed Mom's path back to their room.

I turned to Luke. "I'm sorry," I said. "This house hasn't been the greatest place to be lately."

"Gee, I wonder why?" Luke said, trying to make me smile. When I didn't, he took my hand and we started making baby steps toward the door. When we finally reached it, we stopped and faced each other.

"I finished the poem," he whispered.

I smiled. "Really?" I'd forgotten all about the poem, all about our Fourth of July Celebration in November. Just remembering that night boosted my spirits.

Luke nodded. "It's not with me, so I can't show it to you now. But it's done. I wanted you to know that." He glanced up at the ceiling and then to me. "I tried to show it to you on Thanksgiving Day, but…"

I nodded. "Yeah."

He moved closer to me. "I want to kiss you," he whispered.

My eyelids fluttered and I swayed toward him. Was it possible to have this strong of a pull toward another human being?

I managed to shake my head. "Bad idea."

"I know." He did dare to reach up and lightly move the back of his index finger over my cheekbone, though. "But I thought you'd still like to know."

He was right. I did like knowing.

Chapter Fifteen

I arrived early to school the next morning. Luke was waiting for me once again by my locker. People stared. And they talked. There's no denying that. It was hard to decide which shocked them more: the scandal with my brother or the fact that Luke Carter was interested in me.

He walked down the halls beside me. It felt very strange, like I was wearing my shoes on the wrong feet, but Luke courted like a gentleman. He didn't kiss me in public or even hold my hand. But he subtly let people know he was with me.

I about died when he introduced me to his best friend. I'd lived in the same small town as Nathan Bates my whole life and here was Luke introducing us. Nate very graciously shook my hand, but I had to say, "Hello, Nathan. Have you lived in Stillburrow long?"

He paused at that and cocked an is-this-girl-mentally-stable look toward Luke. But Luke shoved his hands in his pockets and glared at me. "Very funny."

Nate finally realized I was joking and then he couldn't stop laughing.

Luke even had E.T. and me sit by him at lunch. I think E.T. fell into hero worship over Luke too. At first he was a little self-conscious, thinking Luke was making a better grade than he was in trigonometry, so he quizzed him a little. Thank goodness I'd given Luke the head's up about E.T.'s

171

complex. He knew to answer the questions with an, "I'm not really sure." And then he'd scratch his head as if he were puzzled. When E.T. gave him the right answer, he'd nod and say, "Oh, OK. I get it," as if the light was just then dawning. I could've kissed him right there for doing that.

Abby came to school that day, but Sidney didn't. Abby walked down the halls with a limp. I chose to believe what she told everyone when she said she'd hurt her back practicing a new cheerleading routine. But I kept thinking of what Marty had told me and wondering if that had anything to do with the reason she moved like every muscle in her body was sore.

Luke didn't know the whole story about her, but he saw the way I watched her and he constantly tried to divert my attention.

"What'd you get on your trigonometry test?"

I glanced up and wondered if I'd ever grow used to seeing him smile at me. He had a smug grin as he crossed his arms and leaned his back against the locker next to mine.

"You got a better score than you ever have before, didn't you?"

I showed him only the hint of a smile. "Maybe." I closed my locker and strolled away. Knowing he was following, I pulled my test results out of my binder. Within moments, it was snatched out of my hand.

"Ninety-eight percent!" He sounded insulted. I paused and glanced back at him. He'd stopped walking and was holding my test with both hands, staring at it with a gaping mouth. Students streamed around him, heading down the hall in the opposite direction. A few jocks slugged him in the shoulder as they passed.

"I know, I know," I said with a sigh. "You're right. I could've done better."

"Done better?" He glanced up at me. "I only got a ninety-four."

I had to bite my lip to keep from laughing. Stealing the paper back, I spun away and started down the hall again. "Maybe you should've studied more, Carter," I called over my shoulder.

A moment later, I felt a slight jostle at my shoulder. He'd caught up with me again. He was striding quietly beside me and staring straight ahead. His jaw was tense. "Don't even think about rubbing it in," he said.

I shrugged and kept up the brisk pace beside him. But after a few moments of silence, I couldn't take it anymore. "You know, if you start falling behind enough to make Under-the-hill sic a tutor on you, I'll be more than willing to give you a hand."

He glared. "Shut up," he said, then turned away. But he couldn't keep in the laugh. We'd just made it to my next class and he stopped us by the door. He examined my face and then reached up and tucked a stray hair behind my ear. "Good job," he said, and his blue eyes glittered with pride.

I glowed. "Thank you."

"Meet me here, next hour?" At my nod, he leaned over and placed a quick kiss on my lips. I felt my face heat.

Glancing around to see if everyone nearby had stopped to gawk, I couldn't stop myself from lifting a few fingers to my still-tingling mouth. But the only two people that took notice of me were trying to walk around me to get into the classroom. For a moment, I was paralyzed. Why was no one flipping out and staring at me for kissing Luke Carter?

And for the first time, I thought maybe I wasn't such an oddball in school after all. Maybe everyone didn't think I was a freak of nature. Maybe it wasn't so misplaced for me to be seen with Luke. And I couldn't seem to hold back a huge grin.

****

The lake party took place that Friday. I heard

through the grapevine that Abby had asked some basketball player to go with her. It irked me. Sure hadn't taken her long to get over Marty, had it? So I must say I was wickedly pleased when, by the end of the week, Liz Curry had wrapped the basketball player around her finger and snagged him out from under Abby's eager grasp. Abby was forced to go stag with Jill Anderson.

Luke asked me to go with him but I reminded him I was grounded.

"Still?" he said. But he already knew that. He'd been calling every night, asking whichever parent answered the phone if he could come over and see me. And every night, either Mom or Dad would tell him no. I was grounded.

On Thursday, he asked, "How long is this grounded thing going to last?" Then he moved closer and whispered. "I need to read my poem to you."

I grinned up at him. "Read it to me now."

But he only shook his head and glanced around at everyone passing us in the hall. "No," he said with conviction. "We have to be alone."

My eyebrows rose. "Is it that good?"

Again he shook his head. "No."

I punched him lightly in the arm. "You wrote me a bad poem?"

"Shh." He leaned down to my ear. "It's not the best I've written. But it is the most important."

Now I was getting antsy. "Just show it to me so I can read it."

"Nope," he said. "I have to read it to you."

I didn't know whether to be impressed by this stubborn streak of his or to despise it.

I rolled my eyes. "Fine. Whatever. I'll see you when I'm released from Paxton Prison."

But when I asked my parents that night when I was going to be set free, neither gave me a definite answer. I think they planned on keeping me grounded until Luke Carter lost interest.

On Friday morning, Nate wanted to know if Luke was riding to the party with him since it seemed obvious I wasn't going. But Luke remained uncertain. I could tell he didn't want to go without me. And that made my heart go a little wild. I never heard what he finally told Nate. He found me at the end of school, taking my arm and falling into step beside me.

"I'm walking you home," he declared.

We were quiet most of the trip. Other groups of kids, young and old, walked with us for a while. The air was still, but cold. It hadn't snowed yet and the ground looked brown and barren. But with Luke next to me, I couldn't complain. Our hands were locked together and our connected arms swung lightly between us. Every so often our book bags, which were slung over our shoulders, would bump into each other. Luke looked tall and gallant in his letterman's jacket.

As we moved on, fewer people walked with us. We were a block from home before it was finally just the two of us. He moved closer. I knew because I could feel his heat warm me. He bent his head slightly and spoke quietly as if he were talking to the sidewalk:

"Fourth of July in the sky. / Oasis for the night."

I glanced up and was about to ask if I'd heard him correctly, when I realized what he was doing.

"Light explodes like a weeping willow / or a blanket draped over the ground." His walking pace began to slow.

My lips parted as I watched his eyes grow cloudy.

"Bottle rockets and sweet red juice. / Goodbye to innocence and youth." He looked up at me and I noticed a slight red ring forming around his lashes as if the feelings inside were making him misty-

eyed. *"Let freedom flare and sparkle / or picnic under the stars. / It was the cascading color / of an invented Aurora Borealis."*

Luke stopped walking completely then. He turned to face me, taking my hands in both of his. He didn't talk for a moment, and it looked like he couldn't.

And then he finished the poem. *"But the most piercing explosion came from my breast, / when I caught the reflection of rockets in her eyes."*

I sucked in a breath. "I like it," I said, trying to breathe normally. "It's perfect."

Luke's hands squeezed mine. "I named it, 'When I Fell in Love.'"

I stared at him. For a moment I was frozen, unable to respond.

"Carrie?" His voice wasn't quite steady.

I had to blink a few times to bring his face into focus. And when I did, I saw the furrowed brows and worried eyes. "Are you sure?" I whispered.

He shook his head. "I've been so confused about everything lately. I'm not sure about anything." He stepped close. "Except this. You were right. You were right about so many things."

I didn't know if I could take too much more of this gushy talk. My heart was about to overload with all the emotions striking me, so I shrugged. "I usually am."

Luke smiled and bumped his forehead against mine. "How do you do that?"

I looked up at him. "Do what?"

"After that first interview at the football homecoming game, I was so mad at you. I kept thinking up things I should've said but you would've come back with some smart remark. You always know what to say."

He was wrong, but I didn't correct him.

"You were right," he murmured, closing his eyes.

"I didn't want to be seen with you because you weren't a cheerleader or popular, because you hung out with E.T. Fitz."

I pulled away from him and stared up at his face, thinking I hadn't heard him right. He couldn't say this now, not after he'd proven that theory wrong.

"But I couldn't not see you either," he said. "When I went to your dad's car lot and saw you walk out of the shop behind him toward me, something inside me just popped." He shook his head. "That never happened to me before."

"You mean the busted ice feeling," I said.

Luke opened his eyes and looked at me. "So you felt it too?"

I shrugged. He grinned. Then his smile dropped. "I felt so guilty. I was sure you'd figure it out."

"Which I did," I interrupted.

He nodded. "I knew you'd realize I was too ashamed to be seen in public with you but I still wanted to be around you. I'm not sure what I thought I was trying to do. Make some kind of secret girlfriend out of you, I guess. I even tried to make it up to you by telling you about my poems."

"Yep, the poem thing finally caught me up," I said.

Luke shook his head slowly and stepped back. He raised guilty eyes to mine. I thought it should hurt more than this, to hear something like that from him, but when he said, "Do you think you can ever forgive me?" I didn't feel any pain. Instead, I thought about how Luke stood up in the middle of an all-school assembly and defended me to the principal, publicly associating himself with me.

I wanted to throw my arms around him and kiss him all over his face, but being me of course, I had to tease him first.

My hands were still in his and I stared at our

connected fingers for a moment. When I looked up, it was hard, but I managed to keep a stern face.

"Well," I said with a sigh, "I can only think of one thing you could do to make it up to me."

He nodded earnestly and looked ready to do just about anything. "What?"

"You have to let me drive your car."

Luke's face was frozen for a moment and then it broke into the widest grin I'd ever seen. His dimples flashed and his hands broke from mine so he could throw his arms around me and squeeze tight.

"Deal," he said into my ear.

I gripped my eyes shut and hugged him back, letting go of every fear and insecurity I ever had. I don't know how long we held each other there on the sidewalk. But we didn't stop even when a car drove by.

"Take me to the lake party tonight," I said, with my arms still folded around his neck.

"You're grounded," he reminded me.

"So? I'll sneak out."

Fingers tightened in my hair. "No." He pulled back so he could see my face. Then he shook his head. "I'm not giving your parents one more reason to hate me."

"They don't hate you."

But he didn't look convinced. "Ever since they found out about the wine, they can't look at me without glaring."

I bit my lip and touched his face. "I think that's just because of Marty and Abby. Since Marty had a close call, they think they've got to keep tabs on me now."

Luke frowned. "But I won't—"

"I know," I said, holding up a hand. "You don't have to convince me."

He opened his mouth as if to say something, but closed it and sighed instead. Hooking his arm with mine, he turned us toward my house and started walking me home again. "I guess Marty and Abby broke up, then?"

I snorted. "Didn't you notice the way Abby kept asking that basketball player out this week? What's his name? Zane."

Luke shrugged and kicked at a rock, sending it flying off the sidewalk. "Maybe they're just going through a rough time since the misunderstanding over her pregnancy."

I remembered the expression on my brother's face, the complete torture when he looked up at me and said, "They didn't even ask."

"They're done," I said bluntly.

Luke glanced at me sharply. He suddenly jumped in front of me and stopped, jarring me to a halt. "Tell me it's possible they might end up happily ever after. Even if you think it's a slim one, I want you to admit there's a chance."

I tilted my head up to study him. "Why?"

"Because if you admit there's hope for them, then you can admit there's hope for us when I go off to college next year."

My heart shuddered then. I'd been trying to get used to the idea that there was even an *us*. Thinking of next year when I'd be a senior and he'd be away at college was new to me. Now I had a new worry. Great.

"If you're trying to compare us to them, then we're doomed."

Luke squeezed my hand. "Stranger things have happened," he said, trying to be bright.

I bit my lip and glanced down at our joined hands. A month ago, I never would've thought I'd be walking home hand-in-hand with Luke Carter. But here I was, with my Luke, the one who wrote poetry and had a goofy overbite. I tried to focus on the joy of the moment, but he'd ignited this latest concern in me. Were we headed in the same direction Marty and Abby had been going?

"Are you riding with Nate to the lake tonight?" I said instead.

Luke shrugged and stared at the ground. "I don't even feel like going anymore." He looked up. "It doesn't sound fun."

"Well, if you go," I said, "watch Abby Eggrow for five minutes. Then you'll realize how totally over my brother she is."

Luke stopped at the edge of the car lot. He hugged me and then stepped back. "There's still hope," was all he said. He waved to my father who was over by a car talking to a customer, and then he spun away and started off.

I watched him head back in the direction of the school, where he'd left his car parked. I watched him until I couldn't see him anymore. And I hoped as well. I hoped he was right and he'd still be interested in me a year from then.

But the next day, Abby Eggrow was dead. And all hope felt gone.

Chapter Sixteen

We got the call at two in the morning. The sheriff rang, needing Dad's towing service. The phone finally roused me from my dreams the second time it chimed, and I sat up in bed, still drowsy. The light in the hall flipped on and filled the crack under my door. Two pairs of footsteps moved down the hall. And then I heard Mom's voice over the phone.

I crawled out of bed and hurried barefoot to the hallway. When I reached the living room, I saw Dad fully dressed and sitting on the loveseat, pulling on his shoes. Mom paced the length of the living room as she talked to the caller.

"Yes, Georgia. We've just received news from the sheriff. Dean's headed out there now with his tow truck...Oh, no. No!" She gasped and covered her mouth. "I didn't know. I'm so sorry—yes... I'm sure he would...Georgia, just calm down. Everything will be fine."

Mom hung up and hurried over to Dad. "Georgia's girl, Jill, was one of them, Dean. I told her you'd stop by and pick her up on your way." At Dad's frown, Mom clutched his sleeve. "Please, darling. She's so worried and you know she's just going to drive out there by herself if you don't take her. In the state she's in, we'll have another accident on our hands."

I jumped in then, having gathered enough information to make my own conclusions. "What's going on?"

Mom and Dad jumped when they heard my voice but neither answered me. Dad gained his feet and Mom hurried to the closet to fetch his coat. They continued to ignore me as Mom quickly zipped Dad up. When she adjusted his collar, their eyes met. Dad sighed. "I'll pick her up on the way. But she's going to see things she shouldn't have to see."

Mom rose on her toes to hug him tightly.

"Thank you," she said, and walked him to the door. "Be careful, Dean."

Dad turned back to kiss her, and then he was gone. Mom continued to stare out the front door. I came up beside her. "What's going on?" I asked again.

When Mom turned to me, I could tell she'd put on a brave front. But her hands were freezing when she took my fingers. "Carrie," she said in a steady voice, "there's been an automobile accident on Still Road."

"And Jill was in it?"

She nodded.

"Is she OK?"

Mom closed her eyes briefly. "I don't know," she whispered. "The sheriff only told your father it was a bad wreck with two cars involved."

My stomach dropped. If Jill had been in the wreck, it must've been when she was coming home from the lake party. And if she'd been coming home, then she might've collided with someone else also going home. I suddenly needed to know if Luke had gone to that party.

"Who was in the other car?"

Mom shook her head. "I don't know," she repeated in a broken voice. "I have no idea how it happened. I have no idea what Jill was doing out at this time of night. I don't know anything, honey."

"The lake party was tonight."

"What?" My mother's eyes flashed to mine and

then she dragged me into a fierce hug. "Oh, thank God you're grounded." She buried her face in my hair. And that's when it hit me.

"Oh no." I squirmed against her. "No!"

"What is it, Carrie? Carrie?" She gripped my shoulders and pulled me back far enough to see my face.

"I heard Jill was going to go to the party with Abby."

Mom had to sit down after that. Her face drained of color and she dragged me to the couch. We sat together and grasped each other's hands. "I don't think Marty was with her," I finally said.

My mother shook her head. "No," she agreed. "No, of course not. But if it was Abby, then someone's going to call him soon enough." She got to her feet and headed for the phone. "And I'd rather it be me."

I watched her stand in the center of the kitchen, a bathrobe over her pajamas, pressing the phone to her ear, waiting for someone to pick up. "Come on, Martin," she said, starting to pace in her house slippers once again. "Answer the phone."

But Marty never answered.

Mom called once every hour. I knew because I stayed up with her. Even if I would've tried to go back to sleep, I wouldn't have been able to. The phone rang constantly throughout the night as rumors of the accident spread across town. With each call, Mom and I gained another piece of information. First, we found out the Wallaces had been in one car.

Mrs. Wallace had been having stomach pains all night and Dr. Wallace, her husband, finally decided to drive her to the hospital in Paulbrook. It ended up that Mrs. Wallace arrived in the hospital via an ambulance, only to discover she had a bad case of gas. She and Dr. Wallace had come through the wreck OK. One of the two had a broken arm, but that was the extent of their injuries.

When we discovered the Eggrow's car had indeed been the other automobile in the accident, Mom started calling Marty's house every half hour.

Dad didn't get home until six in the morning. By then, we already knew of Abby's death. We knew Georgia was still at the hospital with Jill and that Jill had gained consciousness only an hour before.

Dad was a mess. He collapsed on the couch and didn't move. Mom brought him hot coffee that he drank without speaking. No one mentioned the red stains on his jacket or the trembling in his hands.

When the sun came up, I saw the remains of the wreck sitting in our backyard by the shop. Both automobiles were totaled. Later, someone from Paulbrook's junkyard came for them, but before they arrived, I stared out the kitchen window and saw more than I wanted. I couldn't seem to turn away.

The front of the Wallace's red car was stripped bare. The radiator was dented toward the engine, where the car had T-boned the driver's side door of the Eggrow's Lexus. Red paint streaked the tan finish of the Lexus along with broken glass, and metal so mangled it looked more like crumpled paper. A deflated air bag draped over the front seat like a blanket. I wouldn't go outside to examine the damage, but I stared out at the MADD sticker on the bumper, feeling hollow. I was almost dizzy from the empty light-headedness. Abby Eggrow was dead. It was impossible to believe even as I stared at the proof.

Mom sat by Dad and rubbed his back as he squeezed his eyes closed and tried to forget what he'd seen.

When the phone rang, neither of my parents moved, so I answered it.

"Carrie?"

I closed my eyes and sighed out a relieved breath as I heard Luke's voice.

"Hi," I answered. My voice sounded dull and lifeless...even to my ears.

"I didn't want to call too early," he said. "I was afraid to wake you."

"I haven't been asleep since two."

Luke paused a moment. "So you know?"

I nodded. "Yeah, I know."

"Are you OK?"

Again, I went to the window and stared out at the wreckage. "I don't know," I said. I wasn't sure what OK meant anymore.

Luke blew out a breath. "I still can't believe it."

"Yeah." My eyes closed again. They were starting to hurt. "We don't know where Marty is."

"Really?"

I found a chair at the kitchen table, dropped into it, and rubbed my temples. "Mom's been trying to call him all night. We don't know where he is."

"I could drive around and see if I spot his truck anywhere," Luke said.

My hands started to shake. "That would be nice."

"I'll come over and see you afterward."

"No," I said.

"Carrie." His voice was forceful even though it quivered a little. "I need to see you."

"This isn't a good time," I said.

"Please."

I rested my head on the table and tried to steady myself. "Could you give me a few days? I just...I just need some time to straighten this mess in my head."

Luke said nothing for a time. I didn't think he was even going to respond. But finally he said, "I'll wait." And then he quietly hung up the phone.

I stayed there, with my head down, letting the chilly tabletop cool my cheeks. Dad was finally talking to Mom in the living room. I could hear their hushed voices. Suddenly, I had to get out of there. I had to find my brother. I just had to do something.

I left through the back door and ran all the way to Marty's house. It felt good to have the cold December air rushing through my lungs. When I reached the house next door to the funeral home, I was panting. My ears burned they were so cold and I had a cramp in my side, but I felt better. I felt cleansed.

Marty's truck wasn't parked in his driveway. That was bad news but not surprising. I thundered up the porch and charged inside. In the front room, I found Austin, E.T., and Trevor sitting in a row on the couch. They were watching a funny movie on the television, yet none of them laughed. Three sober expressions landed on me when I threw open the door. E.T. lifted a limp hand and gave me a solemn wave. He tried to smile, but it died before it reached his eyes.

"Where's my brother?" I said.

All three of them shrugged.

"He was gone by the time I got off work this morning," Austin said.

"We can't go home," Trevor piped up.

I stared at him and E.T. explained. "It's a real mess over there. People keep coming in and out and Mom and Dad can't get anything done."

It struck me then that Abby's body was right next door. I shivered.

Where was Marty?

****

The ending words of "Amazing Grace" drifted into the air. Dabbing a tissue at her eyes, Brenda Newell stepped back with the rest of the choir. And Pastor Curry came forward. He stood in front of the closed coffin quietly for a few moments. His Adam's apple slowly slid up and then jerked back down.

It was a Monday morning and tiny flakes of snow were starting to fall. They melted as soon as they hit the brown earth, but it was enough to make everything damp. Wind fluttered the dampness around and small water droplets clung to leaves and coats and faces.

A picture of Abby flittered through my mind: dressed in her cheerleading uniform at the football homecoming, holding her red and white pompoms behind her, stretching up on her toes and whispering into Marty's ear. His lids had lowered dreamily as she spoke to him. In my mind, she would be frozen that way for eternity, with her head close to his and her smile as youthful and bright as ever. I would grow old and wrinkly, and she'd stay that perky cheerleader.

She was John Keats reincarnated:

Fair youth, beneath the trees, thou canst not
    leave
Thy song, nor ever can those trees be bare;

I thought of Marty.

I never found him that Saturday when I'd searched so frantically. Eventually, Mom and Dad set out to look for him too. But he was gone. We worried all weekend until Dad finally said, "He's OK. The boy just needs some time alone, and we should give it to him." So that's what we gave him. Time.

I looked at the flowers surrounding Pastor Curry. Long white lilies with a healthy wet glow sat on top of the box. A smaller bouquet of roses was nestled in the middle of them, and a ribbon ran across the stems, saying, "We love you, Abby" in navy blue letters.

Pastor Curry swept a hand through the air over the casket. "Here lies the body of Abigail Marianne

Eggrow."

That's when it really hit me. My fingers shook as I covered my mouth with them. The wind blew goose bumps onto my arms, but I felt so hot. My stomach revolted and bile rose in my throat. I wiped my nose on my soggy coat sleeve. I don't know if I was being loud, but there was so much weeping and moaning around me, it engulfed me. No one would've noticed a small hiccup from me.

"...And this tragic accident is no one's fault," the pastor said. "Sometimes, the Lord just takes blessed people because they've filled their purpose early. Everyone plays their own song. They sing their story to the world and leave behind a melody of memories. Sometimes...their song is cut short and ends too early. But that doesn't mean their music was any less sweet or that they left any less of an impression."

I bowed my head and squeezed my eyes tight as Pastor Curry said a prayer. *Please find my brother. Please help Marty.*

When I felt a hand on my shoulder, I lifted my face and glanced back.

There he was.

He'd just arrived. His hair was still wet from a shower and his black suit was a little rough, but he'd cleaned up as best he could. His face was pale—so very pale. I moved aside to let him up with our family and he slid in between Mom and me.

I glanced around to see who'd noticed him and found many faces were glancing toward the Paxton boy who'd almost gotten Abby Eggrow pregnant. But to me, my brother suddenly looked tall and handsome.

I was beyond proud of him. I took his hand and his fingers bit into mine because he held on so tight.

I saw Luke then. He was standing closer to the casket than we were, not too far from the Eggrows and the Gettys. His eyes were on me, and when he saw me notice him, he nodded. His mouth smiled encouragingly to me, but there were tears in his eyes.

I heard my brother whimper. When I looked up, I discovered his face was no longer white, but bright red. His lips shook and his nostrils flared as his breathing accelerated. His gaze fixated on the closed casket. Huge drops of moisture gathered at the corner of his eyes.

Mom touched his sleeve and looked up at him with concern. Marty glanced at her, whispering, "I don't think I can do this."

Dad moved from my side and came up behind him. He touched Marty's back and said, "You don't have to be strong, son. We're here for you."

That's all the encouragement Marty needed. He clenched his eyes shut and folded, bending at the waist and letting his head fall forward. Dad caught him from behind before he hit the ground. He turned Marty around and embraced him, fitting his son to his chest and holding Marty's head with his hand. I watched Marty's arms go around Dad and his hands bunch fistfuls of Dad's jacket.

Dad looked to Mom and me then, and we instantly moved in, surrounding Marty in a protective shell. Dad opened his arms enough to gather all of us into his embrace. And right there in the middle of the cemetery—in the middle of the gathering of Stillburrow citizens—my family formed one huge hug and wept together.

I rested my head on Marty's back and listened to his sobs as they echoed through his chest. My parents' arms bound me to them. I had never felt so close to these people I'd shared my whole life with, as I did just then. As my parents cried because of their son's pain, I realized I had never loved them so much. This was my family.

Chapter Seventeen

Marty walked home from the service with us, and Mom and Dad pampered him at the house. Mom poured him a glass of milk while Dad sat beside him on the sofa. Marty thanked them repeatedly, which was unlike him. Mom finally sat on the other side of him and held his hand. Dad chatted with him, taking his mind off the pain.

"Business has been picking up for me in the past few weeks," he said. "I'm getting busy enough I can't handle the workload myself. So I was wondering if you knew of anyone that needed a job. The pay won't be much at first. But I'm willing to be flexible. Do you know of anyone that knows a little about cars?"

Marty glanced up. "You asking me to work for you?"

Dad gave a brief nod. "If you're willing."

Marty mulled it over for a second and then said, "I'm willing."

It was Mom who let out a relieved breath. I watched her as she brushed her fingers over Marty's knuckles. She didn't seem worried about us getting dirt on the floor or what the town might be thinking of us for weeping all over ourselves like we had. It made me feel like she'd changed, like she wasn't so embarrassed to be a part of us now.

It seemed like our family was putting itself back into some kind of order. In the face of tragedy we'd united, and it felt good to know we wouldn't turn our backs on each other when times turned rough.

Marty's eyelids seemed to get heavy, and I think we all realized he needed to be alone. He needed rest and a little peaceful solitude.

My parents had already drifted out of the room and I'd been about to leave Marty alone. But at the call of my name, "Carrie?" I turned back and came to sit by him on the couch.

He looked at me from red raccoon eyes. "Don't tell anyone about what I said the other day...about the baby," he said.

I shook my head. "I won't."

"I don't want anyone to know what I thought. I was wrong, OK?" He waited for me to nod. Then he continued after a shaky breath. "And if I wasn't wrong then she didn't want anyone to know. So I'm not going to let anyone find out."

"OK," I said in a soft voice. "I won't tell anyone."

"I don't think she deserved this," he said.

"Of course you don't." The very idea appalled me.

"But I was mad at her. I tried to hate her. I couldn't, though. After everything she did to me, I still can't. And I didn't want her to die. I didn't."

"I know, Marty. I know." I hugged him.

He bowed his head and raised his hand to his eyes. "She didn't deserve this."

Keeping my arms around him, I rocked us into a sway on the couch. "It's not your fault."

"I didn't know I could hurt this much," he whispered.

I closed my eyes and rested against him. I had no idea what I could do to ease his pain. But after a while, he patted my arm and thanked me. So I guessed I'd done all I needed to.

Or maybe time had done the work.

****

It was early evening when Luke showed up at our front door. Mom let him in. He was looking at

191

her with concerned eyes when I came to the end of the hall and into the living room.

"How are you, Mrs. Paxton?" He said it as if she was the mourning mother of the deceased. It touched me to hear him treat her that way.

Mom smiled at him gratefully and clasped her hands over his. "I think I'm as well as can be expected." Her eyes turned to the door down the hall where Marty's old room was. Then she smiled again at Luke. "Thank you so much for asking, Luke."

He nodded. Mom had already led him into the living room. Dad was out in the shop and Marty was in his old room napping. When Luke saw me, he swept past Mom and came directly for me. Right there in front of my mother and in the middle of her living room, he pulled me off my feet and hugged me so hard, I think I heard my back pop.

He kissed my hair and smoothed his hand down my back. He murmured my name and then he clasped me to him again. "For three days," he said in an unsteady voice, "I've been driving myself insane, thinking what I would do if it'd been you." He pulled back to cup my face with his hands. "I just have to make sure you're OK." And he kissed me again. But this time, he really kissed me.

At first, I was shocked he had the nerve to do this in front of Mom, but then he pulled my mind into the kiss and all I could think of was Luke. He was warm and generous and loving, and I wanted to soak into his warmth where I could hide away until all the pain had passed. And for a moment, I did.

When we stopped kissing, I rested my cheek on his shoulder. He latched his arms around my back and laid his chin on the top of my head. I listened to the low rumble of his voice coming through his chest as he murmured things like how good I felt and how much he'd missed me. I didn't move from his embrace until I heard my father's voice.

I'm not sure when Dad had come in or how long he'd been standing there, but when I lifted my head, there he was, next to Mom.

"Luke," he said, and came toward us with slow, tired steps. When he started saying, "I don't think it's a good idea..." I was ready to jump in front of Luke and fight my parents tooth and nail to let him stay. I hadn't realized I'd missed him so much until he was right there, hugging me. I needed to feel Luke's arms around me, needed to feel alive.

So when Dad finished with, "I don't think it's a good idea for Carrie to be cooped up here all day. Do you think you could take her somewhere for a while?" my mouth dropped. All week my parents had been anti-Luke and now they were begging him to take me away?

What was the deal with that?

Luke slid me a sideways glance that seemed to mirror my shocked reaction. Then he smiled. "I think I could do that."

Dad nodded. "Good. She needs to get out of the house and free herself for a while." He rummaged a hand through his pocket and came up with his wallet. "Maybe you could get her something to eat. Do you need any money?"

Luke lifted a hand. "No. I'm fine." He turned toward me. "I know exactly where to take her."

Mom came up and touched his shoulder. "Thank you so much, Luke. We really appreciate you being here for her at a time like this."

Luke nodded. He took my hand and squeezed. I had to hug each parent before we left and whisper my own thanks into their ears. I was glad they were finally realizing he actually liked me...Carrie Paxton. I was glad I'd finally realized it too.

Once we were outside and walking toward his car, Luke took my hand. "Are you sure you don't mind coming with me?"

Linda Kage

I looked up at him. His concern was so evident, his eyebrows crinkled and his jaw tightened. He'd changed out of the dark suit he'd worn to the funeral and was in his letterman's jacket, a sweater, and jeans. Small drops of snow were settling in his black hair, making it curl around his cowlick. But in the cold of the day, his fingers remained warm around mine.

I couldn't think of anywhere else I'd rather be.

"I don't mind," I said.

Luke opened the passenger-side door for me and waited until I was seated before he shut it. I closed my eyes and pressed my cheek against the cold leather seat. I huddled in my coat, wanting to fall asleep right there and not wake up until all of this was over. When Luke started the car, he didn't say anything, but I could feel him watching me.

I thought he was going to take me all the way to Paulbrook for a meal, so when he stopped the car seconds later I opened my eyes, surprised.

I sat up when I discovered we were parked in a paved circle drive in front of a two-story house with a three-car garage. My heart pounded against my chest and I sent a panicked glance to Luke.

"I want you to meet my parents," he said.

I shook my head frantically, making wide sweeps back and forth with my face. "I'm not ready."

The smile he gave me almost looked sad. "You're not afraid of them, are you?"

I shook my head no, but the word that came out of my mouth was, "Yes."

Luke reached over and snagged my hand. "This is the final step, Carrie. You meet my parents and we'll officially be a couple."

I showed him my doubting look. "There are steps for that?"

He grinned. "Absolutely."

"You are such a liar. And besides, your parents

already know who I am."

Luke sighed and briefly closed his eyes. When he opened them again, he shot me the overly patient look my mother used to give me when I threw a temper tantrum.

"They know who you are," he said, "but they've never actually met you." He shoved his door open. "I'm going to prove to you I'm not ashamed of you, OK? So you have to meet my parents."

And before I could reply, he jerked himself out of the driver's side and slammed the door. I continued to sit there and watched him stop halfway to his front door. Then he spun back to face the Mustang. From my seat, I stared at him through the windshield and read the words he mouthed. "Get out of the car."

I rolled my eyes and opened my door. "Fine," I said, slamming my own door. "Let's go meet your parents." When I caught up to him and was striding along beside him, I added, "So I can prove to you that you *should* be ashamed of wanting to date me."

Luke only glared at me as he pushed open his front door. He let me in ahead of him, and I felt defiant enough to stride inside with my nose in the air. But once I cleared the threshold, the smell of lilacs drifted to greet me and I shrank back, running smack into Luke as he followed me in.

The entrance made Aunt Kay's house look tiny. The floor was a mix of tan and mauve marble for a few feet and then it turned into a smoky gray carpet. Candles flickered in glass sconces on the wall. A huge silver-framed mirror hung next to them, reflecting their light.

"Mom," Luke called from behind me, making me jump out of my skin.

I spun around, ready to retreat. But of course he was blocking the exit. I buried my face in the opening of his jacket. "Don't make me do this," I whispered.

"Shh." Warm fingers settled in my hair. They pressed onto either side of my skull and lightly lifted my head until I was forced to look up. "Will you relax?"

"I'll think about it when this is over."

His blue eyes lit up, and he laughed.

I folded my arms over my chest and harrumphed. "I'm glad you're having so much fun." Then I spun around only to be startled once again.

Mrs. Carter was standing right there. I must've looked like I was watching a horror movie because my eyes bugged and my hand flew up to cover my heart. I could feel Luke's chest shake as if he was silently laughing at me. I stepped back far enough for the heel of my foot to land hard on the toe of his shoe.

The shaking stopped, and I was finally able to smile at his mother.

I saw an amused grin flicker across Mrs. Carter's face as if she knew what was going on. And that made my face heat a little. But then Luke stepped around me.

"Mom, I'd like you to meet Carrie."

My face grew hotter. It felt corny to be so formally introduced to this woman since I'd known who she was my whole life. But Mrs. Carter stepped forward with a familiar smile, a smile that suddenly reminded me of Luke. She had a deep dimple and a bit of an overbite.

"Carrie," she said, and used both her hands to clasp mine. "It's nice to finally meet you, though from the way Luke talks about you, I feel like I've known you for years."

I blinked. "He talks about me...to you?"

"Don't sound so shocked," Luke muttered beside me. I didn't have a chance to glare at him because his mother was leading me further into the house.

"How's your brother doing?" she asked, which surprised me even more.

"He's, uh...He's pretty upset," I said.

"Oh, I can imagine. The dear boy is simply too young to lose someone who was obviously so close to him."

She led me into a sitting room where all the furniture had cherry legs and seated me on a chair with a fluffy cushion and high back. She sat in a matching chair next to me. Luke stood close to the door and watched us with a smirk in his eyes.

"Both of my parents have passed away," Mrs. Carter said, "but they were older and I was prepared for their deaths. I just don't know what I'd do if it happened suddenly to someone I cared for. Your poor brother must be suffering."

"Well, he's...coping," I said. I hadn't expected this at all. I knew people would think about him and stare at him after Abby's death. But I'd expected accusations—not sympathy. I thought they would blame him for making her wild enough to go out drinking and driving.

I didn't know if I could take too much more of this unanticipated behavior from Mrs. Carter. So I looked up toward Luke for help. Could it be possible I'd been wrong all this time?

"I think it's affecting the whole town," he said, coming in to aid me and changing the subject to a less personal tone.

Mrs. Carter nodded, agreeing. "Yes, it's been quite an eye-opener." She took my hands again. "And I thank you so much, Carrie."

I glanced over, frowning. "For what?"

She laughed. "You've completely changed my son."

When my eyes widened, she patted my hand.

"For the better, of course. Before he got involved with you, he would've been at that party and

197

could've been one of those kids in that wreck. But this time, he didn't go and I know it was because of you." Her fingers squeezed mine. "It's about time he found himself a good girl."

When I caught Luke's expression, he rolled his eyes like he disagreed I was good. I frowned at him and then smiled at his mother.

"Thank you," I said, becoming fonder of the woman as the minutes stretched on.

That's when Luke's father found us in the sitting room. He came in stretching and rubbing his stomach.

"Isn't it about time to eat?" He stopped when he saw me. "Well, hello there."

"Dear, this is Carrie Paxton," Mrs. Carter said, rising to her feet and bringing me with her. "Luke's friend."

"Paxton?" At my nod, Mr. Carter lifted a brow. "Why, you must be Dean's girl. I can see it in the eyes."

I risked a quick look toward Luke, but he was no help. I faced the father again and swallowed. "Yes, sir," I said, and tried to brace myself for the worst.

So when he came forward with an outstretched hand and eagerly pumped mine, my fingers were limp with shock.

"Well, it's an honor," he said, grinning.

My eyes grew. "It is?"

Mr. Carter threw back his head and laughed, a laugh that was a lot like his son's. "Isn't she a firecracker?" he said to his son.

Luke beamed.

I jumped when Mr. Carter threw his long arm around my shoulder and led me from the room. "Of course it's an honor. I've always said your father's the most honest man in Stillburrow."

I knew that already, but to realize someone else had figured it out made my mouth drop.

Mr. Carter's chest heaved as he laughed again. "There's no one I trust more to give a loan to. Heck, I'd lend Dean the whole bank if I could. But only because I know he's one that'll pay it back." The man elbowed me lightly in the ribs then. "Didn't know your dad had such good standing, did you?"

I shook my head and felt dumb as I said, "No, sir."

Mr. Carter sighed. "Yes, Dean's a quiet one. But he always gets done what needs doing. You know what I like best about him?"

I shook my head again, completely baffled.

"I like that he doesn't act all hoity-toity like some families around here. By the way some people in this town carry on, you'd think they owned the whole county when none of them have half the investments your father has."

I had to concentrate to keep my mouth from falling open again. Yes, my dad was definitely a quiet one. He'd kept quiet about his "good standing" at the bank so well his own family didn't know what we had.

"Now, come eat some supper with us, Carrie," Mr. Carter said, as he drew me along behind him, "so I can pry the name of this secret poet out of you."

I pulled to a halt. "Secret poet?"

"Oh, yes." Mrs. Carter came up beside us. She looked excited. "We're all avid readers of *The Central Record* here. We're just dying to know who's been writing those beautiful poems."

"Do you like them?" I glanced at Luke before looking at his parents. And the shock I read on his face told me their affection for his poems was news to him.

"Like them? Why, I love them," Mrs. Carter said.

Mr. Carter shook his head. "I can't believe someone from Stillburrow is actually that good. I've

Linda Kage

never seen such talent around these parts. And I don't even like poetry." He pounded a fist to his chest. "But something about those poems gets me right here."

Suddenly, I grinned. "Well, I'm sorry. But I can't tell you who it is." I bit my lip as I glanced from a blushing Luke to his parents. "I'm sworn to secrecy."

****

"I told you so."

I opened my eyes and glanced up. Lying on the Carter's couch with Luke behind me, I pressed my back more snugly against his chest and he wrapped his hand around my waist. Supper had been wonderful. The Carter parents continued their attempt to coax the secret poet's name out of me as Luke played footsie with me under the table.

Yes, I had to admit, I really liked Luke's mom and dad. I'd been so sure they would be snobs and freeze me out. I was glad to be wrong.

After supper, Luke led me into the den so we could rest on the sofa. I closed my eyes, guilty about being thankful I wasn't home where I had to watch my brother's pain.

"What'd you tell me so?" I said.

I was still in shock, but I was quickly getting used to this new state. I wasn't worthless. My family wasn't poverty stricken, and I was good enough to date Luke Carter. I'm not sure how I'd ever gotten myself so mixed up into believing everyone else was better than me. Maybe it had been my mother's own mistaken beliefs that had rubbed off. But I was glad it wasn't sticking.

"I told you my parents weren't that bad and you were worrying over nothing."

I snorted. He felt warm and comfortable snuggled up behind me. "You did not tell me that."

"Oh, yes, I did," he said.

I shook my head. "All you said to me was, 'Get

200

out of the car.'"

"No. That's not what I said." He paused. "Was it?"

"That's exactly what you said."

"Oh, well." I felt him shrug. "I meant to say my parents weren't as awful as you thought."

I laughed and covered his hand with mine, interweaving our fingers. "You're such a liar," I murmured and rubbed my cheek against his.

I felt his smile. "I love you too."

For a moment, neither of us said anything. We simply soaked in the feel of each other. Then turned so I could face him. I rested my chin on his arm. "So much has changed," I said.

Luke reached up and slid a piece of my hair behind my ear. "I know."

"Abby Eggrow's dead and Marty's going to have to get over that." At Luke's nod, I went on. "We're officially a couple." I nestled my cheek against his chest and stared up at the ceiling. "I'm acing my trigonometry tests. And you're the best writer in town. Two months ago, none of that was true. Two months ago, everything was normal."

"Do you wish it were that way again?"

I shrugged. "What's the use? It can't be."

Luke touched my face with his thumb. "But what would you change if you could?"

When I glanced up at him, I saw the uncertainty in his eyes. He was actually worried I would want to change being with him. It gave me a silent thrill to know someone liked me that much, that he really loved me for me.

And I was completely serious when I said, "This may sound awful. But if everything that's happened, happened so I could end up here like this with you, then I wouldn't change a thing."

He smiled and kissed me lightly. When he pulled back, his eyes were shining. "That does sound pretty bad," he said.

I elbowed him in the ribs and he grunted, only to come back and tickle me. I tried to wiggle away and control the urge to laugh, but it ended up we made quite a commotion. Rolling off the sofa in our scuffle, we both landed on the floor. Luke grabbed my wrists, so I couldn't attack him. Then he loomed over me so he could say, "But I feel the same way."

My breath caught in my chest as I stared up at him. He was so beautiful, his nose, his eyes and his dimple—even the scar at the corner of his eyebrow—seemed like they were perfectly placed to make this outstanding creature for me. Luke Carter was destined for great things. And he was going to be by my side through them all.

He'd turned me, Carrie Paxton—the Nobody of Stillburrow—into Carrie Paxton, editor of the school paper. And he was going to turn Stillburrow—a dead-end town in the middle of nowhere—into the childhood city of a famous poet. It suddenly reminded me of Abby Eggrow and history class.

I looked up at Luke. "Ever heard of Appomattox Court House?" I asked.

A word about the author...

Linda grew up on a dairy farm in the Midwest as the youngest of eight children. Now she lives in Kansas with her husband and nine cuckoo clocks. She works in a library and has always loved books: reading, writing, and organizing them. *The Stillburrow Crush* is her first story published by The Wild Rose Press.

Visit her at http:// www.lindakage.com

www.ingramcontent.com/pod-product-compliance
Lightning Source LLC
Chambersburg PA
CBHW071310200626
46813CB00015B/1384